"I have to say, I never thought I'd run into you again."

"There's one thing I've learned in life. Expect the unexpected, good and bad." Especially bad. Although, tonight was the first stroke of luck that made Garrett believe the whole world wasn't against him.

Brianna took another swig of her beer and then set it down. "It's been a long night. I'm done after a shower."

He didn't think this was the time to tell her not to put naked-shower images of her in his thoughts. Instead, he grinned and made a tsk noise. He started to get up, but she waved for him to sit back down.

"Stay overnight?" she asked, a hint of pleading in her voice.

"I've got nowhere better to be," he said. It was probably a bad idea to sleep over. He'd already compared most of his relationships to the way she'd made him feel years ago.

TEXAS STALKER

USA TODAY Bestselling Author
BARB HAN

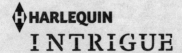

All my love to Brandon, Jacob and Tori,
the three great loves of my life.

To Babe, my hero, for being my best friend,
greatest love and my place to call home.

I love you all with everything that I am.

ISBN-13: 978-1-335-48919-7

Texas Stalker

Copyright © 2021 by Barb Han

Recycling programs
for this product may
not exist in your area.

This edition published by arrangement with Harlequin Books S.A.

For questions and comments about the quality of this book,
please contact us at CustomerService@Harlequin.com.

Harlequin Enterprises ULC
22 Adelaide St. West, 40th Floor
Toronto, Ontario M5H 4E3, Canada
www.Harlequin.com

Printed in U.S.A.

USA TODAY bestselling author **Barb Han** lives in north Texas with her very own hero-worthy husband, three beautiful children, a spunky golden retriever/standard poodle mix and too many books in her to-read pile. In her downtime, she plays video games and spends much of her time on or around a basketball court. She loves interacting with readers and is grateful for their support. You can reach her at barbhan.com.

Books by Barb Han

Harlequin Intrigue

An O'Connor Family Mystery

Texas Kidnapping
Texas Target
Texas Law
Texas Baby Conspiracy
Texas Stalker

Rushing Creek Crime Spree

Cornered at Christmas
Ransom at Christmas
Ambushed at Christmas
What She Did
What She Knew
What She Saw

Decoding a Criminal

Visit the Author Profile page at Harlequin.com.

CAST OF CHARACTERS

Brianna Adair—She is so close to a normal life she can practically taste it, unless a stalker takes everything away.

Garrett O'Connor—This might be the rogue O'Connor, but he would never turn his back on someone in trouble.

Derk Waters—This fellow student is just plain creepy, but is he deadly?

Everett Fulton—This stepbrother is Derk's alibi if he can be believed.

Blaine Thompsett—This grad student might be guilty, or is he covering for someone who is?

Dr. Jenkins—This professor crossed a dangerous line, but is he a deadly threat?

Chapter One

"Thanks for walking me to my car again, Hammer." Brianna Adair waved at Jeff Hamm, a.k.a. Hammer, for his work as a bouncer at the club where she bartended, before sliding into the driver's seat of her Jeep.

"You got it, Brianna. Be careful and remember what we talked about," Hammer said with a wag of his finger. He might be six feet eleven inches of stacked muscle, but on the inside, he was all teddy bear. Unless someone crossed a line. Then, the Hammer dropped and he earned his nickname.

She adjusted the rearview mirror, checking for any signs the pickup truck from a couple of nights ago was around anywhere.

"If the jerk comes back, I go straight to the cops just like before." Cranking the engine, she blew out a slow breath. Since she hadn't been able to get a good look at the driver and there was no plate, the police report she'd filed had been pretty slim. She shook off the fear rising inside her, trying to convince herself that the mystery guy would not return for another round of stressful late-night bumper cars.

Adjusting the mirror again, all she could see as she pulled away was Hammer. The hulk of a man stood in the parking lot with his arms crossed, watching as she safely pulled away from work.

Her nerves were fried, and her pulse kicked up a few notches just thinking about the ordeal. *Determined* was her middle name. Actually it was Jayne but there was no time for reality. Point being, she'd been working at Cowboy Roundup for two years now and there was no way she was letting a drunk cowboy run her off a job that paid better than any other she'd had up until this point. Not that she planned to bartend for tips the rest of her life. Or even the rest of her twenties. If she was still mixing drinks next year, she'd consider the past two years a colossal waste of time. Working late nights in a skintight shirt and Daisy Dukes was a means to an end. And the end was coming soon. Thirty-seven more days. She'd be hanging up her bandanna for a laptop as soon as she finished her associate degree in website design.

She was so close that she could almost feel the nine-to-five. She'd be trading in white tennis shoes for heels and work lunches. So, yeah, she kept on slinging drinks and ignoring comments about her "perfect" backside and the sizable chest genetics had forced on her. Speaking of genetics… She took one hand off the wheel long enough to touch the necklace that had been a gift from her mother, a lucky charm in the form of a four leaf clover. Maybe some of the luck would rub off on her.

With wheat-colored hair and cobalt-blue eyes, Brianna was the spitting image of her mother, save for her mother's bright red hair. Brianna could only hope her physical features were the only things she'd inherited from the woman. After her parents finally landed jobs at a ranch, so the family could be together after her father had spent most of her childhood working an oil rig, her mother had blown the new sense of security by having an affair.

To make a long story short, her parents had divorced but not before a move and a third attempt to "save" the family. So, the small Texas town where she'd tried to finally put down roots had ended up in the rearview faster than a cowboy could say *tequila shot*.

Her parents had given it a good go in San Antonio. The move had been meant to bring the three of them closer together and, if she was being honest, save her parents' marriage. Going into her sophomore year of high school, the tension at home and the stress of the move finally caught up to Brianna. Her grades fell apart faster than her parents' marriage.

At least they'd tried. Now her mother lived in Nashville with the lead singer of a country band. Not long after news of her mother's remarriage circulated, Brianna's father had an accident on the job and, for the next decade and counting, mostly drank while collecting disability checks and basically swearing off women.

So, yeah, her family was rocking it out. Christmases were awesome. And she realized the lucky charm hanging around her neck might not be so lucky after all. A literal sigh tore from her mouth at the bad memories. She loved her parents, don't get her wrong. And she couldn't blame them for trying to hold it together or how badly it fell apart. Many nights, she'd heard them arguing they needed to stay together for her. Marriage. Family. Commitment. Those words caused her to shiver involuntarily in general and made her a little bit nauseous to boot.

She brought her fingers up to trace the charm. The necklace—a sweet gesture from her mother to bring her daughter better luck than her own—reminded Brianna to stay the course in school and at her workplace after bouncing around from job to job. It reminded her that she didn't have to take a traditional route in life and was probably better off if she didn't as long as she didn't crush anyone else's feelings in the process. It reminded her of the love that could so quickly turn to misery.

Brianna had graduated high school. Barely. Not that she wasn't smart, she'd just refused to get good grades. Looking back, she was trying to punish her parents but ended up hurting her own chances of getting into college. Oh, and she'd refused to take college entrance exams, too. So, you know, she was a real rebel. The only person who seemed to be hurting from her acts of defiance was her. She blamed it on the teenage brain, which, in her defense, hadn't been fully developed at the time.

She'd been too stubborn to ask for help, even when she realized she needed it. Besides, her parents had had enough on their plates fighting day and night while getting divorced. That took a lot of time and energy.

Even though her mother had cheated on Brianna's father, it was impossible not to feel like the woman had cheated on the whole family. At the very least, her actions had had a ripple effect. And wasn't that so true in every area of life?

But, hey, Brianna wasn't about to start feeling sorry for herself when graduation was around the corner. She'd managed to get through midterms and then straight through to working on big final projects caffeinated and on very little sleep because she'd had to take extra shifts at the bar recently. Good for her bank account and bad for the bags under her eyes.

A little concealer later, and she was ready for another night. The bartending phase of her life was winding down and she couldn't be happier.

Except that lightning just flashed out of practically nowhere and storm clouds started rolling in. She hadn't checked the forecast in a few days—mistake number one in a place like Texas—but she didn't remember there being any rain in it. The zipper was broken on the door of her secondhand Jeep, Code Blue, named for how many times a month it flatlined on her. Not exactly vintage enough to be classified as a jalopy, her vehicle was so old that it didn't have Bluetooth technology or a USB port. It was paid for, though. And that was all that mattered in a vehicle.

Comfort was optional. Reliability preferred. But complaining did little good to reverse a situation. Trust her, Dad had done plenty of that when Mom had left.

Real change in someone's life took focus and hard work.

The funny thing was that she would have loved driving this beast in the two years she'd lived in Katy Gulch. She could imagine having her friends pile in and go mudding after a good rain.

That was the old Brianna. The girl who knew how to have fun. The girl who had an easy smile, as her wild hair—hair that she ironed now—flew into the wind carefree.

Code Blue sputtered and she thumped the floating gas gauge. Seemed okay but it was hard to tell. Brianna was looking at buying something more modest now as she socked away new-car funds. If she couldn't get something brand-new, she'd settle for new-to-her. Something more conservative. And something that wouldn't let the rain in while she drove to an office job on a nine-to-five.

And speaking of rain, a couple of droplets hit the windshield. Of course. Her time at Roundup was coming to a close and these last few weeks were going to take her for a ride. Well, saddle up, baby, because she wasn't going to let a little water bring her down. There'd been enough wet blankets in her life, and she was so done with negativity.

Famous. Last. Words.

The downpour came on like a tsunami. There was so much rain that her canopy literally ripped a little bit more. Of course, the water came in on the driver's side where she sat, dripping on her face and shirt. She put her left hand up, trying to hold the canopy together so she didn't get flooded.

She shook her head, and rain flew everywhere. So, yeah, more of that Adair luck was kicking in. So much for the charm.

Determined not to let a little rain get to her, she refused to give in. She kept smiling, working hard not to let herself get in a mood. She forced her thoughts away from the jerk who'd pinched her bottom when she'd left the relative safety of the bar to clear a table because her busboy hadn't had a break since he'd shown up. Neither had she, but that didn't count. She could handle it. Her busboy was barely legal and there was no way she was going to work that poor kid's fingers to the nubs.

She could sure use a tall glass of wine about now as she flipped on her windshield wipers, which basically sloshed water around. She needed new blades. The next thing to fail her was the antifog mechanism. All of which she'd promised to get fixed once finals were over.

She needed to make a list of things that she'd been putting off. She'd driven past the dealership every day this week, looking at that powder-blue four-door sedan, thinking how nice it would be when she was no longer at the mercy of Mother Nature as she drove to and from class or work.

Out of the corner of her eye, she saw headlights as she passed Maple Road. A pickup truck sailed around a corner, scaring the crap out of her. The vehicle zoomed up to her bumper, pulling up so close she gripped the steering wheel tighter as she readied for impact. *No. No. No. Not this again.*

Brianna managed to swerve into the next lane when he roared up a second time. She strained to get a look at the driver's face. She couldn't make out who was behind the wheel. She had half a mind to pull over or next to him and give him a piece of her mind except that would qualify her as *too stupid to live*.

Road rage was one thing. This guy, if it was the same one, had come back for seconds. A bad sign.

Instead of going head-to-head with Pickup Jerk, she decided to see if she could lose him.

Come on, baby. She could only pray that Code Blue wouldn't fail her now. A fork in the road was coming up and she figured that would be the best time to make a move. She slowed down enough for the jerk to get close to her bumper again, then pushed Blue as fast as she would go.

At the last minute, she cut the wheel right. The maneuver worked. Pickup Jerk veered left just like she'd wanted him to do.

Before she could celebrate, she saw his brake lights in the rearview mirror. He would catch up to her if she stayed on her current path. Dread settled over her, but she knew exactly what to do. Head straight to the cops. She'd mapped out the closest substation after the last encounter.

This time, she was ready.

"Go ahead. Follow me now." Brianna drove the

couple of blocks to the substation with the truck on her tail. It tapped her bumper a couple of times, jerking her head forward. Whiplash was not going to be her friend later.

This guy needed to have his license revoked. A night in county lockup might make him question his decision behind the wheel.

Her shift had been long. All she could envision was getting home to a hot bath and a soft bed. She was so done with that job it wasn't even funny. So, picking up a stalker in her last month at the bar wasn't exactly high on her list. And she would take this incident very seriously.

As she pulled into the parking lot of the police station, Pickup Jerk must've realized where she'd just led him because he peeled off in a hurry. Not exactly his smartest move, in her opinion.

At the angle she was sitting, his license plate was just out of sight. She almost turned around and tried to follow him except that Hammer had warned her not to do that. After tonight, she might just grab a shotgun and leave it inside her Jeep.

Okay, bad plan. She couldn't even zip the door shut. There was no way she could leave a shotgun in her vehicle. Knowing her luck, Pickup Jerk would steal it and shoot her with her own gun.

So, yeah, that wasn't happening.

Now, the question was whether or not she should follow through with going inside and filing another report. She was so tired that her bones ached and all she could think about was a hot bath and a warm bed.

Nothing sounded better than going facedown on her pillow and it wasn't like she had anything new to tell the officers inside.

Except that this was serious. All her warning bells flared at the fact this man had returned for a second battle. He seemed to know where she worked, and he could follow her home. An involuntary shudder rocked her at the thought.

All right, she decided. She'd go inside and file a report again.

As she sat idling in the parking lot, the hairs on the back of her neck pricked. The feeling of eyes on her caused an uneasy sensation to creep over her. She had the sensation people got when they said a cat walked over their grave.

Trying to shake it off, she glanced around and then checked her mirrors. He might've parked and was on foot because she couldn't see his pickup. Was he watching her? Waiting for her?

With a heavy sigh, she cut off the engine. After zipping up her door the best she could, she checked the back bumper but didn't see any new scrapes or dents. She headed inside the station. Hammer would be proud of her. Actually, he'd be pretty upset that the guy had returned and tried to run her off the road. Creep. Hammer saw himself as guardian of the female bartenders and waitresses at the Roundup. He took their safety personally.

It took half an hour to file a report—for the second time in a week—and fifteen minutes of that was spent waiting to be called to speak to the desk sergeant.

He looked to be a few years short of retirement. Stiff back, hard face and mostly bald. He was thin and tall when he stood up to greet her. He stayed behind the counter as he took her statement. She relayed everything that had just happened as he wrote notes, tagging the new information onto her first complaint.

"Any additional damage to the vehicle?" the sergeant asked.

"None that I could see." The parking lot was well lit.

"Be careful on the way home," he urged with a compassionate look.

"Yes, sir." Best as she could tell, *she* wasn't the problem, but she got what he meant by it and gave him a small smile in return.

"Here's my card. Call if he shows back up tonight," the sergeant said.

"I will," Brianna said, taking the card he'd offered, unable to shake the creepy thought there could be a round two.

Chapter Two

This was routine to the officer, and here Brianna was totally out of her comfort zone as she exited the sub-station. He'd taken her statement and told her to let him know if she saw the truck again. He reminded her not to put herself in vulnerable positions and to stay in well-lit areas if she had to be out at night. He suggested she be aware of her surroundings at all times. She would do all those things. And yet, there wasn't anything comforting about the exchange.

She was still walking away to drive on a near-empty road to an even emptier apartment. Great that she had two incidents on file should this guy come back or do something even worse to her. The cops would be able to lock him away then.

At this point in her life, she had no one at home to make sure she made it there safely. What if she walked into her apartment only to find this guy wait-ing? The police couldn't exactly arrest every single guy who drove a dark truck to ferret out the jerk who was making her life miserable.

It wasn't like she could call someone this late to

come stay with her either. Besides, it wasn't like she had a lot of friends. The past two years had seen her basically keeping her head down and studying. If she wasn't going to class or studying, she was working.

Suddenly, living alone was losing its appeal. She'd always wanted a dog but that was out of the question with her schedule. It would be too cruel to leave an animal home alone most of the day and late into the night. Having a regular nine-to-five where she didn't have to be out on the roads in the wee hours sounded better and better.

Adrenaline had kicked in and it felt like she'd just taken a shot of espresso. So, basically, trying to go to sleep when she got home and settled was going to be fun, if by fun she meant torture. At least she could sleep in tomorrow morning. Thank heaven for small miracles.

At least there was a little activity in the parking lot when she walked to her Jeep. Shift change? Break? She had no idea what a police officer's schedule looked like.

Unzipping the door, she checked the backseat just to be sure. At least the rain had let up. When she saw it was safe, she climbed in the driver's side. The other night when the same thing happened, it had taken hours for adrenaline to wear off. She'd binge-watched Netflix until the sun had come up. By the time she made it to class the next morning, she'd been a zombie.

So, she was none too thrilled for a repeat. Worse yet, this guy really seemed to have it out for her.

She started the engine and checked the gas. The floating gauge could be tricky. It didn't move. She thumped the plastic cover over the gauge and it finally moved...all the way to *E*.

Stopping off at a gas station was now her first priority.

Driving, she was keenly aware of anyone else on the road, especially since other vehicles were few and far between at these hours. She kept checking her mirrors, and her stress levels were through the roof by the time she hit the gas station. She picked the largest one she could find that had plenty of lights, figuring it couldn't hurt to be easily seen by the attendant. Not that she could be picky considering how low her tank was.

As she exited her vehicle and opened the tank, Brianna searched her memory for anyone who stood out at the bar lately. After using her credit card and getting the green light, she started pumping. Whoever was making her life difficult had to have come from work. Right? That was the only place she could imagine, especially since she'd been driving home from the bar both times.

The bar had been hopping and there'd been a few regulars, but that was about it. No one stood out.

What about school? Another brain scan turned up empty. She pretty much kept her head down and tried to draw as little attention to herself as possible. No one had tried to speak to her or ask her out on a date.

A truck pulled into the parking lot and her heart sank. Panic caused her chest to squeeze and her hands to shake. And then the fire came back. She refused to live like this. She refused to be a victim. She refused to cower in the face of a bully.

The driver pulled up opposite her at the pump. And the person who stepped out brought a blast from the past along with all kinds of memories.

"Garrett O'Connor? Is that seriously you?" she asked, grateful for a familiar face even if it had been years since she'd seen anyone from that family or that town.

"Brianna?" He tilted his Stetson and his smile sent warmth washing through her. "It's been a long time."

"It sure has," she agreed. And yet not much had changed. Garrett was still tall and gorgeous. He had to be six foot four inches of solid muscle. Working a cattle ranch would do that to a person. He'd never been the workout-at-a-gym type. He was more of a get-his-hands-in-the-earth person. He was also part of one of the wealthiest cattle-ranching families in Texas. "Do you live here in San Antonio?"

"Just passing through," he said, and she realized that his answer was pretty cryptic. Not that it mattered. Why he was in town was none of her business and he was the least creepy man on the planet.

"Wow. I can't believe it's you. How long has it been?" She willed her hand to stop shaking.

Nothing got past Garrett. He studied her with eyes that bored into her, leaving a fiery trail in their wake.

"Everything all right?" he asked, his dark, masculine voice trailing all over her.

There was no use lying to him. And, besides, what

were the odds she would run into an O'Connor at a gas station in the middle of the night? And it was Garrett no less. The guy she'd dated who'd also broken her teenage heart. They'd only gone out a couple of times but the minute he'd learned his brother was interested in her, he'd backed off big-time. The man was honor and cowboy code to the gills.

A coincidence like this one couldn't be ignored. It was too random and that made her feel like maybe talking to him again was meant to be. And since she needed to be honest with one person about just how freaked out she was, she said, "No. Actually. It's not."

GARRETT O'CONNOR BLINKED a couple of times just to make sure it really was Brianna Adair on the other side of the gas pump. There she stood in all her glory, basically five feet five inches of beautiful sass and wit. She'd been a real heartbreaker in the past, and it was surprisingly good to see her again. Being a decent person, he couldn't let her comment slip past without offering a hand if she needed one. "Anything I can do to help?"

Garrett and his brother Cash had been born fighting. But Brianna was a huge part of the fallout that Garrett had had with his other brother Colton years ago. Colton was happily married and living in Katy Gulch, Texas, with his new wife and twins. The incident with Brianna was water under the bridge by now.

"Do you mean that, Garrett?" She stared at him with the most beautiful set of serious cobalt-blue eyes. Her straight wheat-colored hair fell past her shoulders and he couldn't help but miss the freewheeling curls that used to be there. The slicked, straight hair still framed her heart-shaped face perfectly. And those pink lips—lips he had no business staring at but sure had enjoyed tasting as a teenager. They'd shared one kiss but it had become the benchmark for all others. And there'd been something about those loose wild curls trailing in the wind that spoke to the heart of her true spirit.

"Wouldn't have said it if I didn't." He had no idea the trouble he was about to get into but for every second she hesitated, he figured the ante went up a few more chips.

"How much time do you have?" She put a balled fist on her right hip.

"I make my own schedule if that's what you're asking." He sized her up as he took a step closer to see if she'd been drinking. He didn't think so based on the person he'd known in high school but people changed and a lot of years had passed since he'd known her.

"Can I ask what you're doing out this late at night?" he asked. Looking into her eyes, ignoring the electrical impulses firing away like stray voltage, he got the impression she was spooked by something or someone. A quick glance around said there weren't many other vehicles on the road. A boyfriend? A husband? An ex?

"I just got off work." She shifted her weight and bit down on the inside of her cheek. That move transported him back to high school. It was also her tell that she was outside her comfort zone.

"And? What's going on, Brianna? I haven't seen you in years and, excuse my saying so, but you look like you've either seen a ghost or done something that's making you scared to go home. Bed is where most folks are this time of night." He'd always been honest to a fault. It was another reason his and Colton's relationship came to a head more often than not. So much so, Garrett had decided a long time ago that it was better he did his own thing rather than work on the family ranch—a cattle ranch that was worth hundreds of millions with associated mineral rights. He was part of a legacy, but he'd always had the need to carve out his own future rather than have it neatly lined up and sorted out for him. Call him unconventional but he had a bone-deep need to create his own life rather than be handed down a fortune for hitting the genetic lotto.

"I could ask you the same question," she fired back after a thoughtful pause.

"What?"

The gas pump clicked in her left hand. She nearly jumped out of her skin. Quickly, she pulled it out of the slot and then replaced it. She leaned her forearm against the tank and said, "Like you said, it's the middle of the night. Why are you here in San Antonio? Plus, don't you live in Katy Gulch?"

"Me? Nah." He noticed how she'd turned the tables. It was easy to see that she needed help, but could he get her to be straightforward enough with him to figure out what that meant?

Chapter Three

"I'm here. Talk to me."

Garrett was right. He was there and it should be easy to talk to him. So, why did the words clog in her throat every time she tried to open her mouth to speak? She knew him. Or, at least she used to be friendly with him.

Friendship wasn't the right word for what had happened between them, though. They'd been close at one time and the chemistry between them sizzled enough to set the gas station on fire even as teenagers. That same draw to him that she'd felt years ago—that same sense of being safe and having someone who would look out for her—had caused her to be honest a few moments ago when he'd asked, when she should've said she was fine and let him be on his way.

"Want to come to my place for a cup of coffee?" she asked, shifting her weight to her other foot. The nervous habit from high school stayed with her to this day.

"Will you tell me what's really bothering you if I

do?" He was playing hardball with that devastating show of straight white teeth.

"Yeah, sure."

"Is there someone I should be worried about at your place, Brianna?" he asked. He didn't come across as worried about being able to handle himself so much as mentally preparing in case there was a fight. Garrett had never backed down from a bully and she figured he wasn't about to start. There was a lot of comfort in knowing that some things could be counted on to stay consistent in a world of change. She also realized why he'd seemed so concerned about her.

"Oh, no. It's not like that. I'm not seeing anyone who would do anything like…who would hurt me in any way." The words came out in a rush. What could she say? She didn't want Garrett to think her judgment in people had lapsed to the degree she'd get involved in an abusive relationship. Granted, abusers could be pretty tricky and not reveal themselves until it was too late. But, that wasn't her situation.

Despite the fact her parents had gotten into some pretty heated arguments, there was never any threat of physical violence. Words hurt and there was no excuse for some of the things they'd said. But slaps and bruises had never been part of their deal and she was grateful for that much at least.

"Good." That one word sent a thrill of awareness skittering across her skin. It was more the way he said it. It was the hint of relief that she wasn't in a relationship. Goose bumps prickled her arms. The dark edge to his voice that had a way of washing over her probably caused them. Even at fifteen, he'd had a low timbre to his voice that stirred warmth deep inside and feelings she couldn't begin to know how to handle at a young age.

All of which she didn't need to notice right now, especially after she'd invited him to her place. Of course, she could chalk it up to nostalgia or the fact he had the kind of cowboy code that said he would step in front of a bullet to protect someone he cared about. The fact was probably even more appealing under her present circumstances.

Which actually reminded her that she might be asking him to step into harm's way. He deserved to know the truth so he could make a determination as to whether or not he actually wanted to follow through with going to her place.

His nozzle clicked. He replaced it on the stand and finished his transaction.

"So, Garrett. I should tell you that someone tried to run me off the road earlier. The reason I'm out so late is that I work as a bartender and some creep has followed me from the club twice now." Hearing the words, remembering, brought back the terror of the incidents. Sure, in the moment she'd been reasonably calm, but they had rattled her. She wasn't eager for a three-peat.

"Good to know. Doesn't change the fact I plan to

see you home and take you up on that cup of coffee, though."

Relief was a flood to dry plains. "Okay then."

The muscle in his jaw ticked, a sign he was working up to anger. He'd always been a little hotheaded when they were younger, usually around his older brother. The two had been gasoline and fire. She'd always felt a little guilty for choosing one brother over the other when she should've walked away from the attraction to Garrett. It would've made her life a little less painful because he'd broken her teenage-crush heart, ending the relationship before it really got started.

She'd known Colton had liked her. And he was a great guy. Everyone loved Colton. Girls lined up to ask him out. But she only had eyes for his rebellious younger brother. She should've realized she'd been playing with fire. When two brothers liked the same girl, it rarely ever ended well. And since hindsight was twenty-twenty, she also realized she'd been the one to end up hurt.

It was safe to say everyone had moved on from the situation. Her mom's affair had been exposed a few months later and then Brianna's life solidly went downhill from there.

Remembering all that made her realize just how far she'd come since then. She couldn't help but feel a burst of pride at how well she was pulling her life together in the past few years. The sacrifices would be well worth all these late hours at the bar. Plus, this dirtbag making her uncomfortable would move on too.

All she had to do was keep under his radar a few more weeks and she'd be home free. The best scenario would be for him to take a hint and move on.

"Ready when you are," Garrett interrupted her thoughts. "Which way are we headed?"

"Hand me your phone and I'll put in my address in case we get separated." She held out her flat palm.

He fished out his cell, unlocked it and placed it on her opened hand. She took the offering, and then added her cell number and home address into his contacts.

"I'm sending myself a text, so I'll have your number. Okay?" She glanced up and saw the way he was looking at her. His appreciation caused her heart to skip a couple of beats. She was reminded of the popular saying, *old habits die hard.* Falling for him was an old habit. One she didn't need to repeat. Could they be friends? She could use a few of those in her life right now but she'd start with one.

"Sure." His voice came off as nonchalant, but his eyes told a different story. They'd darkened, intensified as he studied her.

She wondered—hoped?—she was having the same effect on him as he was on her. Because being anywhere in the vicinity of Garrett was electric. A small smile upturned the corners of her lips. Even after all this time an attraction still surged. She had to hand it to him, he looked even better than he had before and that was saying a lot.

Handing back his phone, their fingers grazed and more of that electricity sparked. It was good to see Garrett again. A blast from the past, for sure. But also, it reminded her that she could feel like this for someone again.

Was it too good?

GARRETT LOCKED GAZES with Brianna as their fingers touched. Electrical impulses shot up his hand, vibrating through his wrist and leaving a sizzling trail up his forearm. Did she feel the same?

With the way she pulled her hand back, he'd think she just touched a lit campfire. The corners of his mouth turned up the second it dawned on him why. He shouldn't be surprised. They'd had that same mix of attraction and chemistry years ago and the only reason he'd walked away from it then was because of his brother.

The fight the two of them had had when Colton had walked in on Garrett and Brianna midkiss had been epic. The divide that had been growing between them for years became an impassable chasm that day.

Hell, Garrett hadn't known his brother had taken a liking to Brianna. Not that he could blame anyone for noticing her or wanting to be around her. She had one of those magnetic personalities that most people described as lighting up a room. Her smile…forget about that. It had a devastating effect, reminding him that he had a beating heart in his chest. Then and now. Not much had changed there.

Her parents worked and lived on a neighboring

ranch until her mother's affair—an affair that had lit the town's grapevine when it was discovered who was involved. A deacon, who was very much still married at the time, and Mrs. Adair, also married, had been exposed when his wife had walked in on them in her home.

The Adair family relocated shortly after, but the two years Brianna had lived in Katy Gulch had breathed life into Garrett. Their breakup had been the right thing to do after finding out Colton had had feelings for her long before she and Garrett had met. It hadn't felt good then to end the relationship despite the circumstances and the memory was still sour.

"The address is there," she said on a shrug. "But you can follow me."

He glanced at his phone, memorizing the address. Despite his reputation in school for being the O'Connor who got mediocre grades, he had a photographic memory. School didn't hold a lot of interest for him, so he did just enough to get by. All he cared about was being outdoors, taking care of the land, and his freedom. Being told what to read and when, or what to study and when, had only turned him off a formal education.

Besides, there was a lot to be learned taking care of the earth and not every smart person lived with their nose in a book all the time. Reading was fine. He enjoyed it. Having someone else's taste pushed down his throat was something else entirely.

Garrett climbed into the driver's seat of his pickup

and navigated onto the roadway behind Brianna's Jeep. The spare tire had a cover that read Code Blue.

What could he say? It made him chuckle. Seeing her again brought up all kinds of dormant memories and feelings. Strange, those weren't normally things he paid much attention to. There wasn't much point in stirring up the past. Tension between him and Colton was usually thick, but that wasn't anything new. The two of them had been on better footing recently, though.

Since their father's murder, all of the O'Connor sons had rallied around their mother, as it should be. She was one strong human and he had nothing but admiration for Margaret O'Connor. She was the rock of the family, always was and always would be. She loved her boys and the feeling was mutual. She also did more for the community of Katy Gulch than any mayor ever could. She ran more charities and spent more time helping others than doing anything for herself. She'd brought up six very strong-willed sons, and she held her own against them.

If he read, it was because of his mother. Countless times he'd discovered her in her personal library where she loved to spend her free hours. Family. Community. Books. Those were the things she held dear. But it was the daughter she'd lost that had marked her, marked the family for sadness. No matter how festive a holiday or how much she smiled, there was always something missing. That something couldn't be filled by her husband or any of her sons. The loss of her little girl, her firstborn, wasn't something Margaret O'Connor had ever gotten over.

A house on KBR, Katy Bull Ranch, had been built for each O'Connor sibling, including Caroline even though their mother knew full well the likelihood Caroline would ever set foot in it was next to nil.

Margaret O'Connor clung to hope of her daughter's eventual return even to this day. Garrett couldn't blame her. He had no idea what becoming a parent was like and didn't have the desire to learn. Kids were great for some people. He'd seen his brother, Colton, fall head over heels for his twin boys from the minute they came home from the hospital.

Kids and Garrett?

He almost choked on the idea. Gripping the steering wheel a little tighter, he also thought about the shame it was that his father had gone to his grave without ever finding out what happened to his only daughter.

With the way both investigations were going, the family might never uncover the truth. He realized that his hold on the steering wheel had caused his knuckles to turn white. No matter what else happened, he couldn't allow his mother to suffer. She deserved to know what happened to her daughter, and her husband's killer belonged behind bars.

Brianna turned into an apartment complex that had three buildings and one large parking lot, about half with covered spots that were numbered. Her hand came out the driver's side window, pointing toward a sign that said Visitor Parking to the left. There were half a dozen empty spaces, so he grabbed the clos-est one.

Most people wouldn't hesitate to call him mis-guided for being here on a whim after a chance meetup at a gas station of all places. Since *bad idea* was basically his middle name, he jumped at the op-portunity to help Brianna out. She wasn't exactly a stranger.

But then after all these years, did he really know her anymore?

Chapter Four

Brianna parked her vehicle and then waited for Garrett. She leaned her hip against the side and crossed her arms over her chest, in a lame attempt to stave off the goose bumps that rippled up her arms as he walked toward her. His strong, masculine presence was even more difficult to ignore the closer he got to her. The breeze carried his spicy scent, blasting her senses and stirring her heart. Had he smelled this good back in the day?

She cracked a smile at the thought. Yeah, he sure had. But they weren't at her apartment to reminisce about the old days. A cold shiver raced down her spine at the thought someone could be watching them now.

No. No. No. He couldn't have followed her home. She'd been too careful.

Before the thought could take seed, she wrapped her arm around Garrett's and led him up the stairs and to her apartment.

"Mind if I throw on some dry clothes?" Brianna said as they entered. She closed and locked the door behind them just in case. The extra precaution would help her relax a level below panic. Having Garrett here sent conflicting emotions raging through her from excitement to a sense of calm she hadn't felt in far too long.

"Be my guest." He extended his arm toward the hallway. An emotion flashed in his eyes that she couldn't quite put her finger on and decided it was best for both of them to ignore.

"I'll only be a sec. Kitchen's that way." She pointed even though it was obvious in the shotgun-style apartment. "Make yourself at home and feel free to put on a pot of coffee."

"Will do." The amusement in his voice caught her off guard.

She held her ground. "What's that look all about?"

Garrett really laughed now. "You always were a strong woman. Good to see not much has changed."

"I'll take that as a compliment," she quipped, unable to hide how pleased his statement made her.

"Good. Because that's how I intended you to take it." He didn't wait for a response. Instead, he brushed past her toward the kitchen.

Brianna turned on her heel and headed toward her bedroom with a grin. Didn't seem like much had changed with Garrett either. He was still that same tall, gorgeous and strong-willed person as before. She drew a surprising amount of comfort in the thought.

Yoga pants and a T-shirt seemed too dressed down for company. After peeling off her Daisy Dukes and button-down shirt, she threw on a fresh outfit. Standing in front of the mirror gave her a glimpse at black eyeliner that had run down her face.

Nice.

She traded the drowned rat look for a freshly washed face, applied a light coating of lip gloss and ran a brush through her hair. Or, at least she *tried* to. Her kinks were back and she didn't have time to mess with it.

The smell of fresh-brewed coffee convinced her she'd done enough primping. The one-bedroom apartment lacked space and the decor in the bedroom could best be described as exploded laundry basket. This place was nothing more than a temporary stop.

Taking a step into the kitchen where Garrett came into view caused her throat to dry up. She tried to blame her reaction on allergies.

"How do you take your coffee?" Garrett asked, holding up a mug.

"A little cream, but I can get it." She crossed the room in record time but he still managed to beat her to the fridge. Granted, her kitchen was small and he was standing right next to it.

He poured the cream into the mug. "Tell me when to stop."

"That's good." She only liked a tiny bit and he nailed it. The smile he rewarded her with did nothing to calm her racing pulse.

He replaced the milk carton and she got a good look at his backside. Nope. Nothing had changed there either. If anything, he was getting better with age. By the time he turned around, she'd forced her gaze into her coffee mug before taking a sip. The burn in her throat a welcome change from the dryness moments ago.

Brianna reached with her free hand and rubbed her temple. "I've been on my feet all night. Mind if we take a seat?"

"Not at all." Garrett's easygoing nature was another draw to him. Of course, he could snap to fire and frustration in two shakes but she'd rarely seen that side to him. He seemed to reserve that for his older brother, bullies and people who were mean to animals.

She walked to the round table with a pair of chairs off the kitchen, and sat down. The breath she exhaled released some of the day's tension.

"What do you know about the mystery guy from the bar?" Garrett asked, taking the seat across from her.

"Nothing. I have no idea who it could be." She shrugged before taking another sip.

He studied her for a long moment, as if judging whether to press her on this, then said, "I was surprised to find a coffeepot in your kitchen. Seems like everyone's doing pods now," he mused.

"I had one of those contraptions but I missed the smell. There's something about a pot of coffee on the warmer. It fills the whole apartment, which admittedly doesn't take much. Plus, I like to be able to walk over and refill my cup without any hassle, especially when I'm studying." She risked a glance at him. "Weird, right?"

"Not to me." The words came out so casually she believed him.

"Really?" she asked anyway.

"Half the reason I stopped off at a convenience store gas station was to get a cup of coffee tonight from a coffeepot. There is such a thing as too long on the burner, though, and you just saved me from burnt coffee."

"Are you on a road trip?" She could admit to being curious as to why he was driving around so late.

"Kind of. Not really. Chasing down a lead about…" He stopped and shook his head.

"What?" she asked.

"Nothing I want to talk about right now. Besides, I'm here for you not—"

She was already shaking her head before he had a chance to finish his sentence. "Oh, no you don't. I don't want to talk about me until you tell me what's going on."

Garrett took a slow sip of coffee. He squinted at her like he was trying to analyze whether or not she was bluffing, so she folded her arms across her chest.

"I'm investigating a lead on my father's murder."

Brianna gasped and her chest squeezed.

"I'm so sorry."

Garrett had heard those words more times than he could count and not once had they felt like balm to an aching heart. Until now.

He chalked his reaction up to shared history and didn't put too much stock in it. "Someone used my father's credit card in San Antonio and I aim to find out who since it might be connected to the person who killed him."

"What happened to your father? When did he…" She brought her gaze up to meet his and it felt like all the air was suddenly sucked out of the room.

Garrett had to break eye contact and take another sip of coffee to focus on something besides the way her sympathetic gaze reached inside him, touching a place he never left vulnerable.

"He was killed on our ranch and left for the animals to…" Again, he had to stop and take in a deep breath.

"Who would do such a thing to your father? He was a great man, Garrett."

All he could manage was a quick nod of agreement. "We're trying to figure that out as we speak. My brothers have been tracking down information and several have returned to the ranch full-time to devote to the case. Four of my brothers have recently gotten married or engaged. Turns out, Riggs and I are the only two still single."

"Wow." Wide eyes, mouth agape, she didn't bother to hide her shock. "What kind of timeline are we talking about here?"

"It's only been a short time since Dad's murder." He took in a sharp breath. "If I'm honest, I still can't believe he's gone."

"I couldn't be sorrier, Garrett. I mean those words," she said earnestly.

"I know you do and I appreciate you for it." He had no doubt in his mind she was being sincere.

She reached across the table and touched his hand. Electricity jolted through him from the point of contact. He tried to absorb the effects of her touch rather than give away his reaction. And probably did a less than stellar job of it.

"Your mom must be devastated," she continued.

"She is, even though she's trying to put on a brave face when I talk to her," he said.

"She's a strong person but this is a lot for anyone to try to cope with." She gripped her mug a little tighter and he could see the news was impacting her. She'd been around his family years back and probably knew them better than most.

That was a long time ago, a little voice in the back of his mind reminded him. A lot had changed.

"Between Colton's twins and Renee and Cash's daughter she's—"

"Not so fast. Colton is a father?" she asked. Brianna's interest in Garrett's brother shouldn't feel like a knife stab in the center of his chest.

"Yes. As a matter of fact, he has twin boys," Garrett supplied, eyeing her to gauge her reaction.

"That's fantastic news. Is he happy?" She was oblivious to the pinball-machinelike reaction in his gut.

"He's newly married and seems so," he supplied.

"Anyone I know?" She smiled so hard she practically beamed.

"No. Someone from college. No one knew her.

She wasn't local. Her name's Makena." He shouldn't care that she was checking on his brother, except that she'd been the reason for the long-standing rift between Colton and him, a feud they'd only recently called a truce to.

"I'm so happy for him." She smacked the flat of her palm on the table. There was a glint in her eyes that hadn't been there earlier. "He deserves all the happiness in the world."

"Agreed." He hadn't meant to come off as curt. Trying to say something to soften it now would only draw more attention to it. He hoped she'd let it slide because he felt stupid trying to explain why he was jealous of his very married brother.

She eyed him a little cautiously as it then seemed to dawn on her why he might be testy. She was the reason for the tension with his brother Colton, and they'd only just begun to repair the rift.

"And your other brothers? How are they doing?" she asked, changing the subject. He took note and appreciated the shift.

"As well as can be expected under the circumstances," he supplied.

"Right." A wall just came up and her smile retreated.

"I'm here to find out more about you and your situation." Redirecting the conversation back to her caused all the spark to dull in her eyes.

"What can I say? I'm working on my degree and the countdown there on the wall is how many days I have left as a bartender." She pointed to the handwritten number on a torn-out calendar page featuring today's date that had been pinned to a corkboard that hung on the wall.

"You're getting closer," he said.

"Not close enough if you ask me." She issued a sharp sigh. "And now that I've picked up a creep, the day can't get here fast enough."

"Why not quit early?" he asked.

"Not everyone is sitting on a trust fund," she quipped.

He almost laughed out loud. He hadn't touched a penny of his family's money. "I'd be offended if I didn't know you better."

"Yeah, I heard how that sounded as it left my big mouth. Sorry. I know you never planned on leaning into yours. The funny part is that you don't even want it."

"I'd rather make my own way in life," he said, which didn't mean he didn't appreciate everything his parents had been doing for him. Garrett had always needed to prove to himself that he could live on his own if need be. He didn't want to get used to the trappings of always having food on the table and a comfortable bed.

"And I've always admired you for it. But if I was you, I'd take the trust fund in a heartbeat." Brianna laughed and it was musical.

His heart took another hit. One he wasn't sure he could recover from.

Chapter Five

Brianna never thought she'd see the day Garrett O'Connor would be sitting in her tiny apartment. And yet, there he was. It proved whoever was in charge up there in the sky had a sense of humor.

"I'd give you my trust fund in a heartbeat except that you wouldn't take it," Garrett retorted.

Little did he know she'd consider it now that she was older and knew how hard it was to put herself through college. She would have refused when she was young and naive. But all these months of sacrifice were about to pay off and she had no plans to let a scumbag from the bar stand between her and her freedom.

"Try me," she teased, trying to lighten the mood. It had gotten heavy again when the subject of money came up. And, no, she wouldn't let him pay for her college or rent. Despite being tired and a little more than freaked out by the creep, she had a lot of pride in doing this for herself and not depending on anyone else.

Graduation was going to be a big accomplishment.

One she'd earned on her own without anyone else's help. And she could almost taste the freedom a real job would bring.

"What are you going to school for?" Garrett nodded toward the stack of books on the bar-height counter separating the living room from the kitchen.

"Web design," she supplied. "I'm planning to work a nine-to-five job with a cubicle, paid lunches and vacations, and a dress code that doesn't involve showing off the girls."

"Sounds like hell," he quipped. "Except for that last part."

Brianna blushed. It wasn't something she normally did, so it threw her off-balance. Was he jealous? And why did her face heat at the thought?

"It might not be your cup of tea but I'm tired of working all night for tips, slinging drinks. A normal life sounds pretty good to me right now." She motioned toward her feet. "Just ask my dogs how tired they are and how much they bark every night."

"You've never been one to shy away from a tough task." His voice held more than a hint of admiration, and more of that heat crawled up her neck. At this rate, she'd turn into an inferno right before the man's eyes.

"Thanks for saying that, Garrett."

"So, tell me who you *think* is stalking you," he said in more statement than question.

She shrugged her shoulders. "I don't know. That's a tough one. There's a guy in one of my classes who creeps me out. I'll be taking notes furiously in class only to get a weird feeling like I'm being watched and then look up to see him staring at me intensely."

"Has he come around the bar?"

"A time or two," she admitted.

"Is he alone?"

"As far as I can tell. He never has worked up the courage to come talk to me so he takes a table by the dance floor and nurses a beer," she said.

"Any idea what his name is?"

"Derk Waters, I think. I overheard someone say that in a group project when his team was next to mine. By the way, there should be no group projects in college. I end up doing all the work and have to hear complaints from everyone in the process," she said as an aside.

Garrett chuckled. "Maybe you should learn to let others pull their own weight."

She blew out a sharp breath. "And risk a failing grade? No, thanks. Besides, I tried that once and ended up staying up all night to redo someone's work because they slapped their part together."

"Sounds like something you'd do," Garrett said.

"What's that supposed to mean?" She heard the defensiveness in her own voice but it was too late to reel it in.

"You always were the take-charge type. I'm not surprised you'd pull out a win in a terrible situation."

Well, she really had overreacted. She exhaled, trying to release some of the tension she'd been holding in her shoulders. "Thanks for the compliment, Garrett. It means a lot coming from you. I mean, your opinion matters to me."

"No problem." He shrugged off her comment but she could see that it meant something to him too. He picked up his coffee cup and took another sip. "Okay, so we have one creep on the list. What about others?"

"I wouldn't classify this guy as a creep necessarily but he has followed me out to the parking lot at school more than once. He's a TA, so basically a grad student working for one of my professors. He made it known that he'd be willing to help if I fell behind in class," she said.

Again, that jaw muscle clenched.

"Doesn't he take a hint?"

"Honestly, he's harmless. The only reason I brought him up was because we were talking about school and for some reason he popped into my mind. He's working his way through school and I doubt he'd risk his future if he got caught," she surmised. "Plus, this person is trying to run me off the road."

"You rejected him. That could anger a certain personality type," he said. "What's his name?"

"Blaine something. I don't remember his last name." Up to this point, she hadn't really believed the slimeball could be someone she knew. A cold shiver raced down her spine at the thought. "I've been working under the assumption one of the guys at the bar meant to get a little too friendly."

"We have to start somewhere. I believe my brothers would say the most likely culprit is someone you know. I've heard them say a woman's biggest physical threat is from those closest to her. Boyfriend. Spouse. Someone in her circle." He shot a look of apology. "It's an awful truth."

She issued a sharp sigh. "I can't even imagine who would want to hurt me."

GARRETT WAS ABOUT to ask questions he wasn't sure he wanted to hear the answers to but decided to lean on his brothers' experiences in law enforcement. "Is there someone special in your life?"

"Like a boyfriend?" Her face screwed up like she'd just been sprayed with lemon juice.

"Yes." His gaze dropped to the third finger on her left hand. Relief washed over him when there was no band and no tan line.

"No." She shook her head so hard he laughed. "Wait, it's not funny."

"Your reaction was kind of priceless," he said by way of defense.

She blew out a breath, a move she'd done more than once in the short time they'd been together. She was like a teapot set to boiling over if someone increased the heat on the burner. "Okay, fine. Go ahead and make fun of me."

"Hold on a minute." He put his hands out, palms up, in the surrender position. "That's not at all what is happening here. Don't misunderstand."

"What, Garrett? That I'm alone and haven't dated anyone interesting in longer than I can remember because I also haven't dated in longer than I can recall." Her cheeks flamed and it wasn't like her to get embarrassed. He'd hit on a touchy subject and needed to backpedal.

So, he took in a slow breath before responding, not wanting to fan the flames.

"First off, there's nothing wrong with being alone. I can't tell you how many hours I spend that way, preferring my own company to most." He met her gaze to make sure the flame in her eyes was dimming, not intensifying. Then, he said, "And secondly, you're going to school and working so it sounds like your schedule is too busy for much in the way of free time."

"That's right." Her voice calmed a few notches.

"I didn't mean to insult you and I apologize if I did." Real men said they were sorry when they offended someone. It was a basic tenet for an O'Connor. Finn O'Connor, Garrett's father, had been one of the most stand-up men a person could hope to meet. Garrett wished to be more like his father but that job was reserved for his brothers. In fact, Garrett had always been the one to buck the system. If he could take some of his actions back now...

There was no use going down the road of feeling guilty for something he couldn't take back. His brothers were the "good" O'Connors. Garrett had been the disappointment. *Whoa. Where did that come from?*

Rather than analyze the sentiment, he refocused on Brianna.

"Thank you. Sorry. I'm the one who is being testy." She gave a sincere look.

"Under the circumstances, I'd say you're doing better than you think." He meant it too. Someone had tried to run her off the road twice in a short period of time. "You know, now that I think about it, this has to be someone you know. Or, at least, someone who knows you."

She studied her coffee mug before taking another sip. "What makes you say that?"

"He came back a second time."

A shiver rocked her body. He reached across the table and covered her hand with his in a show of support, but all he did was cause more of that electricity to rocket through his hand and up his arm.

"I feared the same thing." She nodded and then shrugged. "It's just my luck lately." She flashed a glance at him. "I'm not feeling sorry for myself, just frustrated. I'm getting so close to graduating that I can almost taste it. You might not think nine-to-five is heaven, but try slinging drinks for a couple of years in a shirt that's a size too small and shorts I can't wear into the grocery store on my way in to work for fear of a public indecency charge."

He studied her for a long moment without talking. "This job must mean a whole lot to you for you to be willing to put up with all that."

"It does. And it means a fresh start." This time, when she studied him, he was the one who could feel the heat. "I'd been planning to move back to Katy Gulch."

"Really? Most young folks can't wait to get out so they can be around more people their own age."

"I see that and understand it on some level. Not me. Katy Gulch was the last happy memory I had growing up. I figured I could get a job in Austin and move close to home. Besides, you know me. I've always been a private person who needs her space. If nothing else, living in San Antonio has taught me how much I value distance between me and my neighbors." She pointed to the left. "These guys like to wake up early in the morning and…" A red blush crawled up her neck. "Say *hello* very loudly first thing. I mean, good for them, but their bed is pushed up against that wall."

"Sounds awful." Maybe not for the couple next door but for everyone around them. This was one of many reasons Garrett had to have space. He couldn't imagine sharing a wall with anyone, especially someone he didn't know.

"I wouldn't call it the highlight of my morning," she said with half a smile.

"Not the kind of alarm clock I'd want to hear."

"What about you?" She turned the tables on him. "Do you still live in Katy Gulch?"

"I'm in the process of moving back, but, no, I don't technically live there for the time being," he admitted.

"Why not? You have an amazing family and I just thought by looking at you that you're still a rancher." One of her eyebrows arched.

"I am."

"Then, you're going to have to spell it out for me because I'm not following." Her face twisted up in a confused look.

"I've been working ranches, just not the one I grew up on."

"Really?" There was a whole lot of shock infused in that one word.

"I needed time to figure a few things out for myself." He'd been drifting, searching for something he couldn't quite put his finger on.

"And did you?" Her honesty was refreshing, but also a reality check.

"No. Can't say that I did."

"Then, did you move back home to figure it out?" she pressed. There was something about Brianna that made him want to keep talking. Anyone else and he would have told them to mind their own business after the first question.

"Not really. I came home because my father died, and my sense of time changed. I thought I had all the time in the world to figure out my life and come back home with all the answers. Much to my surprise, I didn't and I don't." He expected to glance up and see judgment in her eyes. Hell, he deserved it. Most looked at him that way once they realized he belonged to one of the wealthiest cattle ranching families in Texas but came to work for someone else.

Brianna set her coffee cup down on the table, stared him in the eyes for a long second and then pushed to standing. "I'd say you need something stronger than coffee after an admission like that."

Before he could say another word, she was at the icebox retrieving two bottles of beer. She walked over and set one down in front of him. She located a bottle opener next and within a few seconds, both caps were off.

"To figuring it all out someday." She held her beer out across the table.

"Or not." Garrett clinked bottles before taking a swig. Despite his bad-boy image, he wasn't a big drinker. He also wasn't a womanizer either but once a reputation took seed he'd learned a long time ago that arguing to change people's minds only embedded the rumors deeper.

Brianna's lip curled on the right side. She tilted her head like she did when she was really thinking. "You know what? I'll drink to that too."

Again, they clinked bottles and then took another sip.

"I have to say, I never thought I'd run into you again, especially not at a random gas station in San Antonio of all places," she said.

"There's one thing I've learned in life. Expect the unexpected, good and bad." Especially bad. Although, tonight was the first stroke of luck that made Garrett believe the whole world wasn't against him.

Brianna took another swig of her beer and then set it down. "It's been a long night. I'm done after a shower."

He didn't think this was the time to tell her not to put naked shower images of her in his thoughts. Instead, he grinned and made a tsk noise. He started to get up but she waved for him to sit back down.

"Stay overnight?" she asked, a hint of pleading in her voice.

"I've got nowhere better to be," he hedged. It was probably a bad idea to sleep over. He'd already compared most of his relationships to the way she'd made him feel years ago. He didn't need to make it worse.

Then again, their brief…*whatever*…happened a long time in the past. He'd most likely built it up in his mind to something grander than it deserved. He'd been a teenager full of hormones back then. They were most likely the reason no one could measure up to Brianna since. And not that they'd shared a brief moment of something truly special.

And even if it was true, spending a little time with her might just dispel the myth. Shatter the pedestal he'd placed her on. A voice in the back of his mind argued he'd placed her there so he could have an excuse to leave a trail of broken hearts.

Was that true?

Chapter Six

Brianna woke to the sounds of movement in her kitchen. She sat ramrod straight and glanced at the clock. Much to her horror, it was barely past seven in the morning. She shot out of bed and grabbed the bathrobe on the hook.

Last night came crashing down on her. The fact that Garrett O'Connor was standing in her kitchen, looking all sizzle and chest hair at an obscene time of day, dawned.

"Morning," she mumbled before disappearing to brush her teeth and splash cold water on her face. The shirtless image of the grown man he'd become stamped her thoughts. Great. She wasn't ever forgetting the image, was she?

At least he was hotness on a stick, and the first kiss she'd compared every other to since she was a teenager. All the poor men she'd dated since didn't have a chance against Garrett. He was just the right amount of rebel and recklessness. His heart was pure gold if he let someone in and she knew that was a rare event. Not like blond-haired Pete who was a software engineer, had already bought the house he planned to bring his bride home to and had asked her to stop by his home on the second date to give decorating tips. She got the feeling almost any woman would do. Like he was filling a position and if someone met the base requirements of being reasonably attractive and intelligent the job was theirs.

There wasn't anything special about dating a guy like Pete.

If Garrett asked a woman out, she could rest assured he saw something in *her*. She didn't fit a certain type or description. He was looking for someone unique and wouldn't fall "in love" with the first decent date who ticked all the boxes.

Walking out of the hallway and into the kitchen, her stomach performed a flip-flop routine. The man was seriously hot and it was so much more than a carved-from-granite chin or those steel-colored eyes. The broken part in him was a magnet to the broken part of her. His sense of humor that bordered on being dark spoke to her, made her laugh. If half of what he said came out of any other person's mouth, she'd be offended and rightfully so. She understood what he meant and how he meant it on a most basic level. His words could touch her like no one else's ever could.

And there was something about a man who never needed anyone else. Garrett had been a loner from the day she first met him. She tried to fit in while he didn't care one bit if he did or not. He wasn't looking for acceptance from anyone.

Untouchable? Even if he stuck around, it wouldn't

be for long. He would always need to be on the go, alone. It was just his nature.

"Hey," she said as he studied his cell phone.

"What are you doing up so early?" he asked as she bit back a yawn.

"I'm not used to someone being in my place overnight, I guess." She tried to shrug it off but noticed the corner of his mouth quirked a smile.

She decided it would be best not to ask what that was about.

"Coffee is fresh. Can I pour a cup for you?" he asked.

"I should get it myself. Don't want to get too used to having someone do things for me," she said before thinking.

He feigned disappointment, clutching his chest in the most dramatic fashion. "Mind if I use your shower?"

"Not at all." Her body reacted with a mind of its own; a dozen butterflies released in her chest and sensual shivers skittered across her skin. But, wait… how? "Do you need me to wash your clothes while you—"

He motioned toward a duffel bag. "I brought it in while you were asleep and didn't want to wake you." He flashed eyes at her. "Sorry about that, by the way."

"Don't worry about it. You were doing me a favor by staying here. I'm a light sleeper but I was out longer than usual."

Again, he couldn't or didn't bother to hide his smirk.

"I won't be long," he said, setting down his coffee mug and walking over to his duffel. He picked it up and motioned toward the bedroom. "This way, I take it?"

"Down the hallway and first door on the right. It connects with the master bedroom," she said, pouring a cup of coffee so she wouldn't be tempted to stare at his strong back.

"I did some thinking last night and I'd like you to make a list of anyone you've been in a fight with lately, male or female. Any disagreements qualify. If you've had words with anyone—" he motioned toward the table "—jot them down and we can talk about a plan moving forward."

She liked the sound of those last words, especially the *we* part, but she couldn't ask him to stop his investigation into his father's murder on her account. She nodded, though, knowing full well he wouldn't shift course now that his mind was made up. Garrett was a mule when he wanted to be.

Thinking about his father caused her heart to sink. The realization that he was murdered was a physical blow. Finn O'Connor had been such a good man. He was an incredible father and husband. Mr. and Mrs. O'Connor seemed to have the perfect marriage despite the tragedy that struck early and would have torn most relationships apart. The family didn't deserve this.

She fixed her coffee and then moved to the table. She checked her cell phone. Although she wasn't certain why she bothered. It was good for making calls and the occasional message from one of her parents. But that was about it.

Taking a sip of coffee, her curiosity got the best of her. There had to be a news article about Mr. O'Connor's death. He was one of the most famous cattle ranchers around. A family like his made news.

She set her mug down and performed a quick search. Yes, there was an article all right. She skimmed it but there wasn't much more than the details of where he'd been found and that the family would have a private service.

There was mention of their daughter, Caroline, who'd been abducted from her bedroom on the second floor of the O'Connor family home. When Brianna searched for Caroline O'Connor, she saw that a recent attempted kidnapping case had been linked to the family tragedy, but nothing came of it and the case was closed after learning the mother's ex was behind the attempt. The case involved Cash O'Connor, who was now a US marshal.

Brianna hadn't stayed up with O'Connor family news, so it came as a shock to learn Cash had gone into law enforcement. Garrett had mentioned earlier that a couple of his brothers had. She skimmed *related articles* and learned that Colton had become sheriff of Katy Gulch and its surrounding counties. Again, wow.

She shouldn't be surprised that several of Garrett's brothers had joined law enforcement given they were all honorable people. Maybe it was the fact she figured they would all work at the ranch someday. Speaking of which, there had to be a story behind

Garrett refusing to work for the family business. One he wasn't telling her.

Lost in thought, she was caught off guard when she looked up to find him standing at the entryway, studying her. She'd been so distracted she forgot to listen for the spigot.

"Everything okay?" he asked.

"Yes." She forced her gaze away from a rivulet of water as it rolled down his muscled chest.

He stood there in not much more than jeans. His T-shirt was slung over one shoulder like a towel. His feet were bare. Awareness caused warmth to ripple through her. Her throat dried up and words escaped her.

She took a sip of coffee to ease the dryness in her throat.

"I was just distracting myself." That part was honest enough. Before he could ask a follow-up question, she steered the conversation back on track. "I thought about this as I fell into bed last night and it's creepy to think someone I know might be responsible for trying to chase me off the road."

"Maybe you don't know them well. It could be someone in passing who is fixated," he said.

The word *fixated* didn't sit well either. "We can't go interrogating every person I come into contact with, so where does that leave us?"

"We start with what we know and interview the names you gave me last night," he admitted. He walked across the room and refilled his coffee mug before joining her at the table. Before he sat down, he spun the chair around and slipped his shirt on. *Shame*.

"And the list we make this morning?"

"We go there too," he said.

"We don't even know if this guy is coming to try again. He might just go away after last night. And if not, this could take days or even weeks to investigate, Garrett. I can't tie up your time like that. You were heading somewhere last night. Somewhere I stopped you from going and you said it had to do with your father's investigation. I don't want to be the one who holds you up from that." She had her elbows on the table and was running her finger along the handle of her coffee mug, too afraid to look up at him while she spoke. She didn't want to see anything there that would convince her to let him stick around.

"I hear what you're saying. I'm basically chasing my tail when it comes to my father's investigation. I need to feel like I'm doing something, keeping busy."

"What about your home? Why not just go back to the ranch?" she asked.

"Because I don't want to face my mother one more time without bringing home some answers. My dad died without ever knowing what happened to my sister. None of us has been able to figure it out. Although, admittedly, I've been a little busy doing something else."

She shot him a look and he put his hands up in the surrender position.

"Okay, I'll admit it. I've been wallowing in my own self-pity just a little bit, but I'm ready to go now.

I don't plan to stop until I find something and I can't go home without answers. I can't look my mother in the face and deliver more disappointment." Garrett didn't normally do emotions so the fact he was opening up to her and spilling so much of what he'd been bottling up inside made her sit a little straighter and listen a little more intently.

"I understand." She believed he was being too hard on himself but she understood not wanting to be a disappointment. For very different reasons, she carried the guilt of her parents' divorce for many years before realizing now none of it was her fault. "You're welcome to stay here as long as you like. I'll write down any names that come to mind but I have a lit test later that I have to study for. I have class in—" she glanced at her phone "—a little more than two hours. So, I have to get down to business."

She threw her shoulders back and held her chin up, readying for an argument. Instead, Garrett stood up and asked, "What supplies am I working with in the kitchen?"

He must be hungry.

"I probably have fixins for breakfast tacos if you don't mind using salsa packets from the Taco Shed." She motioned toward a drawer. "There should be plenty in there."

"Breakfast tacos are my specialty."

"I remember," she said quickly, a little too quickly. He didn't need to know just how much detail she remembered about him and the things he was skilled at. The thought of their first kiss caused her face to turn white-hot. She spun around and tucked her chin to her chest to hide her reaction to him—a reaction that was still out of control after all these years and all this time.

"Then, you'll remember how much of a treat you're in for," he quipped without missing a beat. "Why don't you crack open a book and get started while I figure out your kitchen and then feed you?"

"Okay, but I think I'm getting the best part of this deal." Brianna had to admit that it was nice for someone to have her back for a change. She knew better than to get too comfortable in the feeling.

For now, she would do exactly as instructed. Open a book. And marvel that the bad boy of her dreams could cook.

Lit was one of her favorite subjects and she'd wanted to get a degree in English but stopped cold when she looked up salary information. She didn't want to be a teacher and she had no idea what else to do with an English degree. She was handy with computers and could learn anything she put her mind to. Web design seemed like a secure job and she could work for a good-size company.

The paper with two names on it stared up at her. She picked up a pencil and tapped the eraser on the table as she read a dog-eared copy of *Don Quixote*, taking notes along the way.

"You know there's a thing called CliffsNotes, right?" Garrett said from the kitchen.

"Then I won't learn what I'm supposed to from reading the text." She shrugged him off. Even a few hours of sleep had been enough to reset her mood. It had nothing to do with waking up to find Garrett still at her apartment. At least, that's what she tried to convince herself.

The smells wafting in from the next room caused her stomach to growl. Loud.

"Almost ready," he said, dispelling any hope she had that he might not have heard.

Seconds later, he brought over a plate that made her mouth water and a smile to creep across her face. "This is a serious pair of breakfast tacos. I forgot all about the sausage in the fridge. No wonder it smelled so good."

"It's a good thing you didn't point me to flour and ask for biscuits and gravy. Breakfast tacos, I can make." The pride in his voice made her smile even wider.

"Yes, you can." She picked up the fork on the plate and took a bite, mewling with pleasure.

He looked like he was about to say something before thinking better of it. Instead, he whipped up a second plate and joined her at the table.

"*Don Quixote*, huh?"

"Yep," she said.

When he rolled his eyes, she added, "There are people who consider this story the best literary work ever written."

"Then, I'd say they haven't read *The Old Man and the Sea*."

"Not bad, O'Connor. Don't tell me you have a copy in your duffel," she teased.

"As a matter of fact." He made a motion like he was about to get up and prove her right. Then, he sat back down. "Actually, I haven't read it since high school, but I keep it right here." He pointed to his head.

"Oh, yeah? Prove it."

"'No one should be alone in their old age, he thought.'" Garrett's expression turned serious when he added, "Nor go to their grave not knowing what happened to their only daughter."

Chapter Seven

Truths had a way of leaving lasting scars. Garrett pushed his egg around with his fork before finally stabbing it and then taking a bite. There wasn't much he could do besides wait, so he polished off his meal and then finished his coffee sitting on the small patio.

The walls were closing in on him in Brianna's small space and he needed fresh air. Being indoors much at all had never been his cup of tea. Why would he when he could be out on the land, looking up at a bright open sky that went on for miles?

Seeing Brianna again sure hit him in an unexpected place—a place he'd kept buried underneath years of turmoil. There was something about being with her that made him not care if he'd been locked inside for hours. So, he needed to get a grip before he forgot who he was.

Thinking about her situation made him rethink some of his own mistakes. He had a family who cared about him and a bank account with more zeroes than one person needed. Would Brianna let him help her?

Really help her? Like with a scholarship or something? Hell, he didn't know how it worked.

He was a simple man. A good cup of coffee and the great outdoors was all he needed to be happy. Guilt stabbed him when he thought about how hard Brianna was working to make a living and have a future better than her past.

What was his problem?

He'd had a solid childhood. His parents loved him and his brothers were close. Well, maybe not with him. He'd always pulled away from the others and he and Colton were like oil and water. It was probably normal in a large family to have spats but theirs ran deep. There was resentment on both sides. Although, to be fair, Colton seemed real happy the last time Garrett spoke to his brother. Wildly happy. And he'd found what seemed to be real joy with Makena. Garrett was glad for his brother despite a hurt that ran deep.

Their disagreements were habit at this point. Could Garrett change? Be more like the person his family seemed to expect him to be? Not everyone got top grades in school or cared about throwing a ball the farthest.

He'd been compared to his near-perfect brothers for a lifetime. One of the best things about going to work on a ranch and only giving his first name was that no one knew who he was. He didn't come with all the baggage that forced him to try to be perfect all the time.

He realized he was white-knuckling his coffee

mug. Forcing his hands to relax, he flexed and re-leased the fingers of his free hand, trying to work out some of the tension that came every time he thought about his brothers. Colton seemed to be the worst. All Garrett had to do was say his brother's name and he could feel his shoulders tense. What was it about the two of them that made it near impossible to be in the same room?

Was it that Colton always thought he was right? Being older didn't necessarily mean being smarter. Although, to be fair, his brother was book smart. He'd been a decent student whereas Garrett had looked for reasons to cut class. Sitting behind a desk had never appealed to him.

He thought about Brianna's plans to get a nine-to-five job and his finger automatically came up to loosen his collar as it suddenly felt a lot tighter. Then, he realized he wasn't wearing a collared shirt. He questioned the appeal of having someone else tell him when to go to work and when to take a break.

The steady paycheck he understood. Those came in handy when rent was due. Working ranches solved the problem of rent for him because the job always came with a spot in the bunkhouse. With all the machines running ranches instead of hands these days, it only took a skeleton crew to handle the labor. It also made him self-sufficient in the cooking department. No one would credit him with being a restaurant-quality chef but he knew his way around a skillet. Meals were usually part of the deal on a ranch too.

Not for Garrett. He preferred not to get to know his coworkers or break bread with them.

Did that make him antisocial?

Maybe. But it also made him happy. Or at least it used to. *Happy* might not be the right word so much as less frustrated all the time. A question he'd never once pondered struck while sitting on Brianna's patio, watching the sun make its ascent. Why?

He'd never once questioned why he was so angry all the time, or had been. Losing his father had knocked the wind out of him and he felt nothing but numb until now, until seeing Brianna again.

The alarm he'd set on his cell phone buzzed, indicating she had to be at school soon. He'd lost track of time while sitting outside, the sun warming his face.

With an exhale, he pushed up to standing and then grabbed his coffee mug from the small side table. This was all a person needed to be happy, a little sunshine, a good cup of coffee and a person he…

Never mind the last part. He didn't have to go there mentally about the electricity or bond he felt with Brianna and how it created a feeling that he'd been missing out on something his entire life.

Garrett was a whole person. He didn't need someone else to "complete" him. And yet he couldn't deny the feeling of rightness that came with being around Brianna again. Like the out-of-control world righted itself and time stood still. Like he was exactly where he was supposed to be. Like he would feel an emptiness he'd never known when this was over and he walked away.

Pushing through those thoughts, he opened the slider to the patio and stepped inside. "Ready to go?"

Brianna's face pinched as she checked the time. She glanced over at him and for a split second time warped and he got caught in the wave. He was transported back to high school when a glance at her felt like the sun coming out from behind dark clouds.

Giving himself a mental head shake, he closed the slider, breaking the moment. "Don't want you to be late."

"You're coming with me?" She didn't hide the shock in her voice as her wide eyes blinked up at him.

"That I am."

"Oh. Okay. I guess there's a coffee shop on campus you can sit at while I'm in class," she offered.

"Don't worry about me. I'll be fine. I plan to do a little walking around while I'm there. See who I can talk to." He figured the department secretary would be a good place to start if a TA might be involved. From what he remembered about his brothers going to college the admins knew everything that went on in a department.

As far as starting points went, it wasn't a great one, but it was something.

Brianna packed up her backpack. A couple of minutes later they were heading out the door.

"I know you were driving somewhere when I saw you at the gas station but can I ask a serious question?"

"Yes," he said as he claimed the driver's seat of his truck after opening the door for her. And, yes, she was fully capable of opening her own door. However, her hands were full and he was brought up old-school. Since she smiled and thanked him after, he figured she appreciated the gesture.

"Do you always keep a duffel bag full of clothes and toiletries in your truck?" Her question caught him off guard.

"Yes." He started the engine.

"Can I ask why?"

"I always have to be ready to spend several days out on the land when I'm working a ranch. It's habit to be prepared for anything that can come my way," he explained. "Why? Does it seem odd to you?"

"I was just curious," she said but there was more to it than that. He heard it in her voice—a musical voice that calmed his aches more than was wise to allow.

And he knew right then and there she didn't ask the question she really wanted to. He could hear it in her tone. What she really wanted to know was whether or not there was someone special in his life.

After a short drive and a few directions, Garrett parked on a side street and then walked Brianna to class. He needed to find the arts-and-tech building. The campus was small, so it only took a couple of minutes. It was still early for some, he figured. Days on a cattle ranch started around four thirty, so a nine o'clock class was basically midmorning for him. His late breakfast would hold until Brianna finished at her college. She had one subject this morning, a nine o'clock, which meant she'd be done at noon. He would be ready to chew an arm off by then so he made a mental note to swing by the coffee shop and see if they had any protein for him to snack on to tide him over.

In the meantime, a woman named June was his next mission. According to Brianna, June was the person who kept everyone in check in the department. She was also a student's best advocate, helping sort out schedule conflicts and obtaining the right signature when someone needed to get into a class in order to graduate on time.

The arts-and-tech building was an all white structure looking like something that came out of an alien movie. A hill blocked its view from the main part of campus and when he crested, he was treated to a vision of a modern glass structure surrounded by newly planted trees.

Garrett jogged down the hill and then strode with purpose toward the building. Only a couple of stragglers strolled around.

The office was easy enough to find since it was all glass with large white letters etched in the window, Arts & Technology. He could see June sitting behind a desk with piles of papers on it. As much as the world had gone to tech, some people stood their ground and worked the old-fashioned way. He couldn't fault her. He leaned into tradition when it came to cattle ranching too.

June was tiny behind the massive desk, but her movements were fluid and assured. She had on a camel-colored blazer, a shirt that looked like silk and there was a ladybug pin that could only be described as dainty on her lapel.

She was timeworn and had a short curly hairdo that was probably very popular a couple of decades ago. He liked June without even speaking to her yet.

"Hello," he said after knocking at the door, not wanting to surprise her. Although he seriously doubted anything could rattle her.

She acknowledged him with a wave.

He stepped inside and waited by the door while she studied the paper she had in her hand. She wasn't fast but he figured she was accurate. No rushing. No multitasking with June. She opened a drawer, carefully located a slot and slipped the paper in a folder.

Then she turned toward him, gave him a warm smile and placed her palms flat on her desk, elbows out. "How may I help you?"

"My name is Garrett O'Connor and I was hoping to talk to you about one of the TAs working in the department."

June's eyes widened just enough for him to realize she knew his last name. He shouldn't be surprised. Plenty of folks knew the O'Connor name, especially in Texas. But it still caught him off guard because he didn't really get out much. The glint of recognition came when he talked to someone about a job but most dismissed the notion a real O'Connor would be looking for work at a competing ranch. Little did they know no one truly competed with his family's scale.

June recovered quickly. "Are you a prospective employer?"

He studied her, trying to get a good read on her. Was she leading him to ask the right questions so she could respond? He hadn't thought about the ethical dilemma she'd be in or the fact there were probably privacy laws covering the kinds of questions he had.

He stared at June for a long moment and caught the slight nod she gave.

"Yes." He could technically interview the guy for a job at the ranch. He was one of the owners. At least on paper. No one would trust his decision-making skills after he'd gone out on a limb years ago to bring a fellow student into the bunkhouse when he himself was barely thirteen, if that. He'd gotten caught up in a new kid's hard luck story at school.

On Garrett's insistence, the family welcomed the kid with open arms. He'd left with full pockets. Full of Garrett's mother's prized earrings. Full of a sterling silver baby rattle that belonged to Caroline and was his mother's most precious treasure. Shame washed over him at the memory.

Was that when Garrett began withdrawing from the family?

Mentally shaking off the fog, he refocused on June. "Can you vouch for Blaine Thompsett?"

June leaned forward and nodded. "He's a good kid."

There were no seats across from her desk. To the left was a hallway with what he presumed would be the professors' offices. To the right was a seating area for students who were waiting to see someone.

"Comes to work on time," she continued. "Of

course, I don't know him personally but I've never heard Dr. Stanley complain."

"He reports to Dr. Stanley?"

"Yes, that's his adviser. Blaine transferred in from a satellite location in East Texas," she continued. "This is his first semester here so I don't know him as well as some of the others but I haven't heard anything that would make him a bad employee so far."

Garrett wasn't sure how much he could push this conversation with June. She seemed loyal and efficient. Someone who prided herself on her work and work ethic. Getting her to give information about anyone under the table didn't seem likely.

He made up a few routine questions employers had asked him during interviews to keep the visit sounding legit.

"Would you like to speak to Dr. Stanley?" She nodded toward the hallway. "I believe he is in his office."

Since the question seemed to come out of the blue in the middle of their conversation, he took it as a sign she couldn't really speak while one of her bosses was nearby. There could be others too. Her space was out in the open in the middle of all the action. From her spot, she could run interference for her bosses.

Brilliant setup for people who didn't want to be available on short notice. There were a few hard walls but a lot of glass on the inside, as well. From his vantage point, he couldn't tell whether professors were in or out.

This was the first time in Garrett's life he wished

he had one of his brothers' badges. That would get June talking as much as she was legally allowed to.

Turning on O'Connor charm wouldn't do any good either. Not with June. She was straight as an arrow.

"Oh, here he comes now—Blaine." June motioned behind Garrett. He had no idea what to say to the kid.

This whole conversation was about to get awkward as hell.

A tall, thin guy with a runner's build and a backpack slung over his shoulder walked into the office. His hair was in need of a cut and his clothes seemed like they could use a good washing. On some level, he might be considered good-looking; he flashed a casual smile when he saw June.

"There's someone here checking a reference—"

"I'm Garrett." He turned to face Blaine, cutting June off before she could bust him. Garrett stuck a hand out.

Blaine's handshake was weak at best. He tucked his hair behind his ear and smiled. "What can I help you with?"

"Could I have a few minutes of your time?" Garrett asked.

"Um, yeah, sure, why not?" Blaine gave Garrett a once-over. He probably surmised correctly that Garrett was too young to be a parent who'd come in fighting for a better grade for his kid.

"Outside?" Garrett gestured toward the hallway.

"Yeah. Okay."

"Thank you, June." Garrett used as friendly a voice

as he could muster before rushing out the door to preempt June from spilling the beans.

He led Blaine all the way outside and onto the grassy hill. The young guy looked confused. He also looked to be about twenty-three years old and way out of his league with Brianna, but the last part was purely opinion.

Garrett thanked Blaine again for following. "I'd like to ask a few questions if you don't mind."

Blaine pursed his lips together and gave an I-don't-know-why-not look. They were out in plain daylight and that was on purpose so the guy wouldn't be as on edge.

"How well do you know Brianna Adair?" He figured he'd better get straight to it and see how the guy reacted.

"Who?" He shoved his hands in his pockets like a kid being accused of sticking his hand in the cookie jar.

Garrett repeated the name.

"I don't know. Is she a student?" Blaine looked down and to the left, a clear sign he was either lying or nervous. Garrett would double down on both being the case.

"Yes." Garrett crossed his arms over his chest as Blaine rocked back and forth on his heels.

"Let me think." He pulled his hands out of his pockets and used his right to rub the scruff on his chin. He grabbed the strap on his backpack and toyed with the end. "She's in one of my classes?"

"Yes." Garrett waited, giving away nothing of his frustration in his tone.

"Do you mind if I ask why? Did something happen to her?" His forehead creased with concern. The fact that he was stalling didn't sit well with Garrett. There was also the fact that he wasn't admitting to knowing who she was yet. Why?

The simple answer was that he didn't want to be caught hitting on her. That wouldn't exactly look good to his adviser. Self-interest was usually the reason most people dodged answering a question or failed to tell the truth about a situation.

"She's fine. She's in class as we speak," Garrett said.

"Right," Blaine agreed quickly. Too quickly?

"Are you familiar with her schedule?"

Another possibility as to why Garrett would have intimate knowledge of Brianna seemed to dawn on Blaine as he looked Garrett up and down as though sizing him up. Blaine would lose if he threw a punch and he seemed to come to the same conclusion when he surrendered.

"Are you her boyfriend?" Blaine's already white skin paled.

"Let's just say I'm a friend who is concerned about her." Garrett had no plans to budge an inch on giving out any more information about their relationship. Hell, he was having a difficult enough time defining it for himself, especially after that kiss. It wasn't more than a peck on the cheek and yet held more sizzle and promise than any kiss he'd experienced in longer than he cared to remember.

This wasn't the time to think about the kiss.

"But she's okay?" There was a guilty quality to his tone that Garrett didn't like.

"Yes. Why? Is there a reason she shouldn't be?"

"Well, no. I just thought…" He blew out a breath, looking flustered. "If she's okay why are you asking around about her?"

"I'm not asking around. I'm asking you." Garrett caught the guy's gaze and held it, daring him to look away first.

Blaine blinked a couple of times before rubbing the scruff on his chin again. "I know who you're talking about now. Right. Brianna from Design 201. I'm glad to hear she's okay. I don't know how else I can help you, so… I better get to class."

Garrett didn't think this was the time to point out class had started twenty minutes ago. And a question lingered. Why did Blaine suddenly look like a trapped animal trying to escape a cage?

Chapter Eight

Brianna sat in class, tapping the eraser on her note-book. The lecture hall was set up like stadium seating in a movie theater. On most days, they all took notes on their laps. But today was test day. So, tray tables were pulled up and out and notebooks were tucked away inside backpacks.

No matter how hard she tried to focus on the test questions, her mind kept looping back to last night. To the incident on the road and then the strange co-incidence of running into Garrett at the gas station. Life was full of surprises. In her experience, they were never this good.

The fact he'd stayed over caused an unsettled feel-ing to creep over her. Having someone in her corner for the first time in a long time was nice. Too nice? Or just too nice for her? The other problem was get-ting used to it.

Garrett would walk away later today or tomorrow. He couldn't stay at her place indefinitely. Her small apartment barely accommodated one person. He'd in-sisted on sleeping on the couch last night even though there was no way a man of his size would come close to fitting, and forget about being comfortable.

And why was she even stressing about any of this when she needed to be focused on taking this test? Failing wasn't an option. She was down to thirty-six days to graduation.

Could she quit her job early? The sleazebag had to be someone at the bar. That was the only logical explanation considering both times she'd been followed by someone after her shift. Code Blue was an obvious ride so there was no confusing her with someone else.

Whoever was after her was *after her*. Another involuntary shiver rocked her. She tried to blame her response on the frigid AC in the building but with the doors opening and closing every fifty minutes or so very little cool air was locked in. The AC would be different at her professional job. She'd been reading everything she could get her hands on about work environments. She would be prepared for the constant air-conditioning in her nine-to-five. Apparently, office temperatures were set to make men comfortable in suits. She wondered if anyone even wore those on a daily basis anymore, except in a handful of positions. The tech revolution made jeans and sweaters *très* chic for office wear. She'd read somewhere that socks were now a big thing in male office wardrobes. Socks?

To each his own.

Any dress code would be better than the outfit she had to wear for the bar. In an office, she could wear clothes. Sweaters. Long pants. Jeans on casual Fridays. The whole "dealing with coworkers" bit wasn't as appealing because she had no idea what to expect. The one thing she was certain of was that she'd already put up with worse. Much worse. At least her current job had prepared her to deal with all walks of life.

The TA at the front of the room checked her watch. "Ten more minutes."

What? No.

Brianna's heart thumped a little louder as the first person stood up, done with her test. She walked it to the front and then set it down on the table. From the back, Brianna couldn't see if the student was smiling or frowning. First one done could mean either she knew every answer and was prepared or she didn't have a clue and gave up. Brianna couldn't take her eyes off the woman.

The nineteen- to twenty-year-old turned toward the door and Brianna got a peek at her face. Smile.

The next person who stood up was a young guy, thick glasses. He'd been sitting in Brianna's row. Done. Smiling. A trail followed as panic engulfed her. She knew the answers to the test. Concentration was her problem.

Since there was nothing like a deadline to kick her brain in gear, she forced her gaze back to the paper and scribbled faster. Her pencil didn't leave the paper until two seconds before time was called.

When she looked up and saw Garrett standing in the doorway, her heart leaped in her throat.

"I WASN'T EXPECTING to see you so early." As Brianna walked toward Garrett, his pulse shot up with every step she took. He'd been leaning against the door-jamb for all of two seconds before class was called.

"Figured I'd walk you to your next class and see if the creep is hanging around." He hoped she'd be able to point the guy out.

"That's a date, um, deal." A hint of red shaded her cheeks with the slip. She dropped her gaze to the floor. "I feel so old in these classes."

He glanced around and guessed the average age of students was probably still in the high teens or early twenties. "You're twenty-six. Not exactly old."

"Not *this* young either," she added without missing a beat.

"No. I hope this doesn't sound like I'm on a high horse but I'm proud of you, Brianna." He could barely look her way for a reaction for fear he'd just frustrated her.

This time when her cheeks flamed red, his chest squeezed.

"That means a lot coming from you, Garrett," she said, her voice low.

"How'd you do on the test?" He needed to change the subject because, for a split second, this felt like one of the most intimate moments of his life.

"I think I passed at the very least. I'm not the best at taking tests but I have a good grade in the class so even if I bombed I'd probably come out okay," she admitted.

"This is a great thing you're doing. Going after your dreams," he said.

"I wouldn't exactly say I'm doing that." She hesitated as they fell in step together.

"Then, why would you torture yourself going through classes, tests and a job you hate?" He didn't mean for all that to come out at once but he was caught off guard by the admission.

"I want a steady job. I'm decent with computers and I have a creative side I thought I could use with web design." She shrugged. "I'm doing this for money, not to follow my dreams."

"Okay then, what would your life be like if you did that?" It wasn't his business to pry and yet he wanted to know more about what made her tick.

"I'd go after an English degree," she said after a long pause.

"English?"

She tapped his arm with her elbow. "Yes, English."

"You want to be a teacher?"

"Not really. That's the part I'm not so sure about. I have no idea what I'd do with an English degree. All I know is that I love reading pretty much anything I can get my hands on. I scribble here and there but, believe me, my writing is nothing to brag about. Web design is a practical choice and maybe not the most exciting one, but I figure it'll pay the bills and then I can do whatever I want with my free time. Maybe take more English classes or just read." She didn't make eye contact and her tongue kept darting across her bottom lip when she paused, a sure sign she was nervous. And then there was the playful elbow jab. Garrett couldn't count the number of times she'd performed that move years ago before they started seeing each other. "I'm probably just selling out."

"Making certain you can take care of yourself financially isn't the same thing as selling out." Was she afraid he'd condemn her decision? He wasn't one to put someone else's life choices down. Her situation was also putting his into perspective—a perspective that was coming on like a kick in the pants but was needed.

"Are you sure about that, Garrett?"

"One hundred percent," he confirmed.

She stopped in front of a building and put her fisted hand on her hip before he could express all his thoughts. He should be proud of himself. That was the most he'd been able to tell someone outside his family in longer than he could remember. Strange as it was, he *wanted* to talk to Brianna. He was downright chatty around her. And that was saying a lot.

"I better go inside." She pushed up to her tiptoes and planted a kiss on his cheek. "I don't want to be late."

All Garrett could do was stand there for a long moment under the spell of that peck. He'd never had a bigger reaction to something so small in his life. So, it caught him off guard that his pulse raced and his heart jackhammered his ribs. Garrett figured a couple of nights at the club sitting in a quiet corner would give him the vantage point he needed to watch her from across the room, see if the jerk showed.

He leaned against the building, scanning each guy who walked past, searching for any sign of the malcontent. A sea of jeans, T-shirts and backpacks flooded the lawn, dispersing in different directions. He had to give it to Brianna; being one of the oldest people in class couldn't be easy.

Her confession sat heavy on his mind as he figured he'd pass the hour-and-a-half class outside her building while he mulled over his thoughts. It wasn't like he had to be anywhere. He was on the way back from investigating a lead that turned out to be a dead end on his father's case. Distracting himself with Brianna's situation was probably for the best. Focusing too much on one subject never helped find answers faster. In fact, the opposite was usually true. The less he thought about a situation or circumstance, the better, the more his mind cleared.

Brianna also gave him a break from the crushing ache in his chest at the thought he would go home to KBR never to find his father there again. He gave himself a mental slap to refocus.

After talking to Blaine, Garrett couldn't exactly cross him off the suspect list. The guy acted pretty dodgy there at the end of the conversation and never really answered Garrett's questions. The whole part about pretending not to know who she was didn't sit right either. Any guy who went to the trouble to follow a woman out to her car to hit on her in a parking lot would definitely remember who she was. Plus, she was in his class. Why was he acting like he didn't know who she was? It didn't make sense. Why not admit that he knew her from class and answer Garrett's questions straight up?

The guy was guilty of something.

Was he frustrated by her rejection? Blaine seemed the nervous type. Was that just grad-school jitters in general or was he hiding something?

Then, there was the creep. Garrett had a good mind to slip into class and have Brianna discreetly point Derk out. A slight nod was all that was needed. Garrett flexed and released his fingers to get rid of some of the strain. Ranch work was all the physical outlet he needed, so not having his usual workout caused stress to build up in his body. Pain caused his shoulder blades to pull taut. He tried to convince himself that lack of a workout was also the reason for the energy that pulsed between him and Brianna every time they were within a few feet of each other, but he could admit his attraction to her was based on more than overwrought nerves with no release. In truth, the teenager who had been a budding beauty had transformed into an incredible woman.

Life had handed her a difficult situation and she was facing it head-on, doing what she could to better her life. Beauty was more than outward appearance. He could admit hers was stunning. And, hey, a nice package could be pretty great to look at. Except that he also knew from eating out of a chocolate box at Valentine's Day back in middle school that not everything in a beautiful wrapper tasted great. For example, what was up with the strawberry-cream one? Seriously. He'd popped one of those in his mouth in seventh grade and nearly gagged. He'd had to run to the trash to spit it out and couldn't get rid of the taste until lunch.

Outward appearance only got a person so far. Real beauty came from the kind of guts and heart it took to work hard and put herself through school in hopes of making a better life for herself. It came in the form of the sacrifice she made and was making.

Garrett couldn't think of her lack without owning up to his abundance. Money he never touched. Why was it so hard for him to take what his family had worked hard to provide for him?

The easy answer? He wanted to make his own way. Now she had him thinking there was more to it. He'd hopped from job to job, never satisfied for long. The changes in employment he made every few months or year only temporarily gave him peace of mind. It never took long for the same problems to surface again. Garrett was a solid worker until he got bored. Things generally spiraled from there. Disagreements about supplies and how to properly tag and record cattle arose. Or how to treat medical conditions in the herd.

Garrett could admit to being stubborn. And he could be a real jerk when he chose to dig his heels in. His temper was legend and something he wasn't proud of.

Being with Brianna again was shedding a whole new light on life, corny as it sounded even to him. But she was. Watching her work for something she wanted so badly, never mind how awful it seemed to Garrett, stirred his admiration.

A part of him wanted to see what she would do with that English degree if given a chance. Hell, the frustrating part was that he could write a check for a scholarship for her without batting an eyelash. He wouldn't miss the money, especially since he never touched it anyway. The idea of finding a way to help others with his money had been on his mind for a while, but he'd never landed on the right way to go about it. Maybe this was it, reaching out to someone he knew personally.

The tricky part would be getting her to accept it. She wouldn't see it that way. She would see it as a handout. And he was fairly certain she'd thank him before rejecting the offer and sending him on his way. No looking back.

The thought felt like a face slap, even though it shouldn't. What should he care if she refused to take his help and then booted him out of her life?

Because losing her would be a real loss, a little voice in the back of his mind pointed out.

Mind wandering, he heard feet shuffling and the sound of chatter filling the hallway through the open door.

Brianna emerged from the crowd with a frown on her face.

"What's wrong?" he asked.

"The creep didn't show today. When I asked the prof if he knew anything about it, he said no. Another student said Derk wasn't coming back. He dropped the class two days ago."

Chapter Nine

"Did he say why?"

Brianna shook her head. "It was my first question, though."

"Any idea where he lives?" Garrett asked. The fact he was still in the exact spot where she'd left him caused all kinds of fireworks to go off inside. Had he waited there the entire time? From the looks of it, he had. This seemed like a good time to remind herself he was never happy in one spot for long. Of all the O'Connors she could have fallen for back in the day, this was the last one she should have picked if she wanted security. Of course, tell that to a reckless teenage heart.

"No. None," she admitted.

"We might be able to convince administration to give it to us. Of course, this process would go a lot smoother if I had one of my brothers' badges," he said.

"There are privacy laws against the school giving out any information. I've heard kids talk about them, being grateful their parents can't log on and check grades at will." Brianna kept to herself mostly. But she'd had to work in a group from time to time and had heard a couple of younger students talking about being close to failing.

"True."

"Plus, if you had a badge, and I think you mean follow in your brothers' footsteps rather than borrow one, you would be bound by some kind of oath not to use it for personal gain," she continued.

He was nodding as he rubbed the day-old scruff on his chin. After sleeping on her couch and then taking less than ten minutes to shower and clean up, he looked too damn good. She had to spend a whole lot more time ironing her hair into submission and applying light makeup. She hardly wore any during the day because she had to wear more than she liked to at night. A little extra eye shadow went a long way toward covering up her real self.

"What about classmates? Did you ever see him speak to anyone?" he asked.

"Rarely. I don't even think he spoke up that much during groups. I never heard anyone complain about him not pulling his weight, though." She searched her memory for any tidbit that could help them figure out who he was and where he lived before coming up empty.

"There has to be a way." Garrett was stubborn. Always had been and always would be. She had to give him that.

"Yeah, sure. We could hack into the system," she quipped.

Her offhanded remark seemed to resonate as his eyes widened.

Brianna put her hands up, palms out. "Whoa. Hold on there. I wasn't suggesting we should—"

"Hacking into the system is a crime." He cut her off, stabbing his fingers through his thick mane and taking a couple of steps in the opposite direction. When he whirled around, her pulse quickened. "I'm not deluded enough to try anything stupid or illegal. Going to jail isn't high on my list of things to do today."

"Okay, good. Because you can be a little…" She stopped when she saw his expression change. Tension pulled his face muscles taut for a split second and he brought his hand down to his side.

But what was that look that had crossed behind his eyes… Expectation? Hurt? Resolve?

What had he expected her to say? Wild? Reckless?

Those words would all be true and yet saying any one of them seemed like it would have a bigger force than a physical punch. Her chest squeezed and it was suddenly hard to breathe, despite being outside where there was plenty of oxygen. It was like someone had punched her in the solar plexus.

Words were powerful, but so were intentions. What she had intended to say seemed to have had just as much impact. Or worse? Because the flash of hurt in his eyes wasn't something that would have happened with physical pain.

Brianna took a step away. She needed air. She needed space.

"Hey, I gotta take a walk," she said when she could finally turn around and face him again.

"What?" His face screwed up with confusion.

"I need a minute. Okay?" The feeling building inside her seemed like it would burst like a volcano if she didn't put a little more distance between them. The kiss, which had been nothing more than a peck, had crept into her thoughts so many times during class she hadn't been able to concentrate.

Without waiting for an answer from Garrett, she took off in the opposite direction. Failing school wasn't an option, which she would do if he was all she could think about. She refused to allow that to happen, not even for a man like Garrett O'Connor. Not when she'd come this far. There was too much riding on her finishing her degree and getting a real job. The thought of waking up one day, bent over from age, still working at the bar and scraping together money to pay for her tiny apartment shocked her to the core. The tips were good now, but for how long? Definitely not forever. When her youth faded would she be relegated to washing dishes or becoming a barback, assisting bartenders for a living? No, definitely not the last one, not when her arm strength faded. She needed a ton of energy to carry boxes of liquor to the bar let alone all the glasses.

Before she realized, she'd made a lap around the building. Garrett stood there, leaning against the bricks with his arms folded across his chest and his legs crossed at the ankles.

This time, she kept a good eight feet of distance

between them, taking a step back the second she felt the force field that was Garrett pulling her in, making her want more than she knew better from him, from any man.

As Garrett opened his mouth to speak, Brianna's professor stepped out of the building. He was in his late forties, average height with a stomach that hadn't seen a gym in years if ever, and a bulbous nose. His hair was greasy and near bald on top, which he tried to cover with a comb-over. He had large yellow teeth and a ruddy complexion. He took one look at her and frowned.

"Ms. Adair?" He took a step toward her, oblivious to Garrett.

"Dr. Jenkins." She didn't know exactly what to say except that her gut told her to walk him away from Garrett. Or maybe it was just her needing more space. Either way, she started walking in the opposite direction. Garrett held back. She didn't have to look to know. She could feel his presence and taking those steps away from him was like walking into the shade on a chilly morning.

"How are you?" Dr. Jenkins, on the other hand, fell in step beside her.

"Fine." She didn't say anything more than necessary, hoping her prof would split off in a different direction so she could get back to Garrett. As much as she didn't want to get too close to him, she could admit being away from him was much worse.

"Are you certain about that?" Dr. Jenkins continued.

"Yes. Why? Don't I seem okay?" Had she really been that transparent? The short answer? Yes. All she'd had to do was take one look at Garrett to confirm. The hurt in his eyes earlier would haunt her. The last thing she wanted to do was let down someone who was helping her. She owed him coffee. Or dinner.

"You've been...distracted lately in class."

In that moment, she realized he wasn't just talking about *this* moment. Hadn't she always been told she wore her emotions on her sleeve? Wasn't that how her mother used to put it when Brianna was sad or lonely as a kid?

Buck up, buttercup. Being a kid is the best time of your life. Her mother's words echoed in her thoughts.

"I promise you that I'm working hard, sir." Her hand came up to touch the necklace and it caused a spark of resolve not to let her mother's words dictate Brianna's life.

Dr. Jenkins crinkled up his nose like someone had just held a bag of dog poo underneath. "When I hear the word *sir*, I turn around and look for my father. Call me Shram."

Why did this conversation make her feel like she was being sold snake oil? She mentally shook off the sensation. She really liked most of her profs. This one had always rubbed her the wrong way, and yet she needed to play the game with him because she needed a good grade.

Dr. Jenkins took a step closer to her and she instinctively drew away from him, elbow out in case he tried to follow. If she'd learned anything at the bar it was to protect her personal space no matter what.

"We can always do more, Brianna," he said so low she almost didn't hear him.

"Excuse me? What did you just say?" She played like she had no idea, but deep down she had no doubt what the "more" meant to him. She could see it in his leering grin, and then he reached out and touched her arm, giving it a little squeeze.

She jerked her arm back so fast he seemed momentarily stunned by her reaction.

His moment of shock was followed by another moment of hesitation. "Keep at it, Ms. Adair. The semester will be over before you know it. If you find yourself in need of extra credit, my office hours are posted."

Was he kidding her right now?

"To be very clear with you, sir." She intentionally used the word he didn't like because it reminded him their relationship was formal not friendly. "I have no intention of needing 'extra credit' because I work hard and deserve to pass."

Last time she checked she had a B minus in his class, which was more than enough to pass the semester.

His body stiffened as though she'd actually thrown that elbow into him like a soccer player gunning toward the goal.

"I appreciate the advice, though. Make no mistake, I'm taking notes." She gripped her cell phone in her hand, pulled it out of her pocket, and held it up.

"With determination like that, I have no doubt you'll pass the course, Ms. Adair." He practically stumbled over his words as he tried to get them out. He seemed very clear on the implication she'd been recording their conversation. "If I or someone on staff can be of any assistance, don't hesitate to reach out."

The man couldn't seem to get away from her fast enough. He practically tripped over his own feet trying to escape.

Garrett jogged up beside her a moment later. "What did he say to you?"

She turned to look at him and his spicy scent filled her senses. The kiss came to mind, how rough his beard felt in contrast to her lips, and she had to fight the urge to do it again for many reasons. Not the least of which was that her recent experience from moments ago had her wanting to reach for comfort.

Brianna almost laughed out loud at the thought. Garrett O'Connor was strength and excitement. He was high-risk, high-reward material. Until the shine wore off and then he would shatter her heart into a million tiny flecks.

The far-fetched part was that he would never want to hurt her on purpose. She realized that on a deep level. They'd known each other for years. Not the facade people put up. The *real*. And the real that was Garrett was too risky for her. She could fall in love with this man. Soul-fulfilling, rock-out-the-sheets love.

And where would that leave her when he got bored

and needed to move on? He might not even get bored of her…just bored. He never could stick around in the same place for long.

She whirled around on him, wanting a different reality to be true.

"Can I ask you a question?" she started.

"Okay." He drew out the word, clearly surprised based on his expression.

"How many ranches have you worked at in the past year and a half?" She tucked her cell phone in her pocket and planted her balled fist on her hip. Eyes forward, she kept marching toward the parking lot.

"What does that have to do with anything?" His dark brows knitted together.

"It has everything to do with everything, Garrett." Did he really not see that?

He captured her elbow with his hand, stopping her in her tracks. "Tell me how?"

"Answer the question first." She tapped her toe on the ground, unable to meet his gaze.

He let go of her elbow and issued a sharp breath.

"Let's see." He paused like he was counting. The longer the pause, the quicker her heart beat against her ribs. "Five or six."

"In eighteen months?" She didn't bother to hide her shock.

"Is that important?"

"It is to me." She turned away from him and stalked toward the parking lot, leaving him standing there by himself.

WHAT HAD JUST happened here? Garrett planted his feet on the ground. No way did he plan to give in and give chase. Brianna had to be willing to talk to him about what was going on inside her head. Did she think he was a mind reader?

One minute she gave him a peck on the cheek that left a fiery trail and the next she couldn't stand to be in his presence. She needed to decide which one it was going to be. Hot or cold. There was no room for both.

He fisted his hands as her rejection stung again, stronger this time. Garrett seriously couldn't figure out the opposite sex. If he was being honest, he couldn't figure out Brianna. Maybe he should just walk away and leave her to it. She seemed ready and able to push him away at a moment's notice. Meanwhile, he stood there like a lovesick puppy.

News flash. He wasn't. In fact, he didn't even have to be standing here right now. He narrowed his gaze as he thought about getting in his pickup truck, driving her home and then hitting the highway.

Maybe it was time for him to head back to Katy Gulch and face everyone. He'd avoided it as much as humanly possible so far. *And go back with what?* A little voice in the back of his mind asked.

The lead on his father had turned out to be a dead end. His credit card hadn't been used in San Antonio after all, as Garrett had believed after getting a tip. Garrett had no new information to take back with him. He wasn't any closer to figuring out who murdered his own father. Frustration nipped at him like a determined pit bull.

Garrett could always rent a hotel room nearby. His laptop was tucked in a backpack inside his truck, power cord and all. He wasn't much for computers but he knew the basics. He knew enough to order supplies and perform research. What if the person or persons he was looking for lived in Katy Gulch? The annoying little voice picked that time to remind him about Ms. Hubert, the local who was murdered in her front yard. The investigation into her death prompted questions about Caroline's kidnapping.

With a couple of exhales, Garrett's frustration settled down a few notches. He seriously needed a good workout. He could go for a run later. He knew full well he wasn't going to leave Brianna defenseless. He caught himself on the last word. She was far from defenseless but she lived alone and had very little in the way of resources.

After watching her deal with her professor, he had no doubt she could handle herself with any rational person. An out of control one? That was a different story altogether. Someone with a gun? Again, that would give someone an unfair advantage over her. Just thinking about it caused Garrett's blood pressure to shoot up. He'd done a lot of things wrong in his life. He'd quit jobs by walking out, sometimes telling his former boss and sometimes not. He'd binged on alcohol over a weekend or two. He'd bet on the wrong horse more times than he could count. But he never let someone he cared about down.

Period.

Even Colton could always count on Garrett if he

got the message, as frustrating as their relationship could be at times. If Garrett heard his brother was in trouble, he wouldn't hesitate to track down any SOB who'd threatened him or any of his other brothers.

So, why couldn't he track down what had happened to his sister? Why couldn't he give that peace to their parents? Now that his father was gone, there was no giving Finn O'Connor answers. Garrett's mother, Margaret, had to be sick by now with worry after the past had been dredged up as recycled news. Of course, anything an O'Connor did or didn't do was news. Their family was nothing more than entertainment to some folks. An O'Connor's feelings didn't matter, people thought. They had everything other people wanted. Love. A nice home. Money. Two parents who adored each of them. They had everything except peace of mind when they laid their heads down at night. Garrett had spent half of his childhood wondering if the guy who stole Caroline was going to come back for one of his brothers. Him. He'd spent the other half angry the sonofabitch had taken his sister and not him.

From where he was positioned, he could see Brianna. He could see his truck. He could see her standing there with her arms crossed over her chest, tapping her toe against the earth in a staccato rhythm.

Suddenly, she didn't look quite so fierce. She looked like she was putting up a brave front to cover the fact she was afraid.

After a sharp sigh, Garrett threw his hands down to his sides and closed the distance between them.

He marched right past her to open the passenger door before claiming the driver's seat. She stood there as he started the engine.

That woman was the definition of stubborn. She was also the definition of beauty. Confidence. Fire. Intelligence. And other adjectives he didn't want to spend too much time adding to the list.

"You coming?" he said in more of a bark than anything else.

"You leaving?"

"Not until you get your sweet backside in my truck," he said.

"Just go, Garrett." In those three vulnerable words, all his anger melted away. She had her back to him to hide the fact she was crying.

Now he felt like the jerk and he wasn't even sure why.

Chapter Ten

Brianna stood there in the parking lot. Tears brimming. There was no way she was going to cry in front of Garrett. She couldn't remember the last time she'd shed a tear. There were times, in fact, when she wished she could cry just to release all the pent-up frustration inside her. There were days when she felt like she might explode if she didn't find a release valve.

She couldn't remember the last time she'd had sex but her brain screamed *too long*. Forget about good sex or anything that came close to the passion she felt in one little kiss. It wasn't even a real kiss and yet it left her lips tingling for the entire class. She couldn't shake his scent.

"Hey, come on in the truck and let's grab lunch." Garrett's voice normally had the kind of certainty that would make her buy firewood during a Texas summer from him. This time was different. This time, there was none of that usual Garrett swagger. This time, there was none of the confidence that bordered on cockiness. This time, there was a hint of vulnerability.

So, she took in a fortifying breath, plastered on as much of a smile as she could muster and turned toward the passenger seat. Thankfully, the tears welling in her eyes dried up. She wasn't sure if it was pure willpower or a stroke of grace. She'd take either one as she climbed inside the cab and then closed the door behind her. She secured her seat belt without looking at him, tucking her chin to chest to hide her eyes. One glance and she was afraid he'd be able to read right through her.

And she didn't want him to know how thrown she was by what had just happened with him or with Dr. Jenkins. She'd rather put both behind her and focus on who was trying to run her off the road on her way home from work at night.

"We can do this however you want, Brianna. I'm not going anywhere until we see this thing through. But, it would help a whole helluva lot if you talked to me about what was going on. What the professor said that threw you so bad." His words were measured and calm. There was not a hint of accusation or judgment in them. Garrett started up the truck and then put the gearshift in Reverse before backing out of the parking spot.

"I'm pretty sure my teacher just let me know how I could pick up some extra credit, and it made my skin crawl." Her chin quivered but she refused to give in to the emotions pressing heavy on her chest, wrapping around her like a thousand-pound blanket, squeezing the life out of her.

The truck came to a screeching halt. Garrett slammed the gearshift into Drive.

"No. No. No. I don't want you to do anything that could cause me to fail that class, Garrett," she warned, praying he wouldn't impulsively jump out of the truck and find Dr. Jenkins.

"Are you kidding me right now?" Anger caused his voice to shake.

"I know. It's disgusting. Believe me." An involuntary shiver rocked her body. "I think I threw up in my mouth a little bit when he suggested it."

"Tell me his exact words," Garrett said; more than a little heat radiated from him.

"Why? What does it matter?"

"Because I'm going to make him eat every one of them." With Garrett's size and temper, she had no doubt he could take Dr. Jenkins apart limb by limb.

"And then what?" she asked, needing to find a way to calm Garrett down but also appreciating someone having her back for a change. "He'll press charges. You'll end up in jail. I'll fail the class because there's no way I'd be able to go back in there and face him."

"I can't stand the thought of him getting away with something like this, Brianna."

"He didn't," she quickly countered.

"Not with you. But how many other female students has he pulled this on?" His anger seemed to brim just below the surface, and she had no idea how much or how little it would take to make it bubble over.

"You're right," she conceded. "I can't let him get

away with this. But I also have to pass the class. And before that, I have to live long enough to figure out what jerkoff is trying to make sure I end up alone in a ditch in the middle of the night. Right now, Dr. Jenkins is the least of my problems, so you have to let me handle this on my terms."

Garrett issued a sharp sigh.

She turned to face him and saw his jaw muscle clench so hard she thought he might crack his back teeth. "You have to promise me you won't do something…" She searched for the right word.

"Stupid?" There was so much fire in that word, it was as though someone had poured gasoline on a raging fire.

"No." Stupid was the last word she would come up with when it came to Garrett.

"What then?" He turned his face toward her with wild eyes. "Out of control?"

She was shaking her head furiously but it didn't seem to make a difference in the state he was in. "I don't think you are any of those things, Garrett."

"Are you sure about that?" Now he was looking at her like he was murderous Jack from *The Shining* at the moment he lost his mind.

And yet, not a fiber of her being was afraid of him. So, she crossed her arms over her chest and said, "You can look at me like that all day but I know you, Garrett. I don't know what you've been through in the past few years to make you think other people might view you like that from the outside. All I can tell you is that I know personally that you are none of those things. Impulsive? Yes. Stubborn? A mule has nothing on you. But you are not stupid. And you are certainly not out of control."

"If you know me so well then why don't you tell me what I really am?" Some of the fire receded from his voice.

"Give me a minute to think and I'll tell you." She didn't need a minute. It was a stall tactic to force him to slow down. Counting to ten in moments of stress and frustration had gotten her through many a fight.

"Well?" More of his anger faded.

"Incredibly smart, for one. You can make me laugh and it doesn't even seem like you're trying all that hard." She'd keep the part about him being smokin' hot to herself. "I'm not worried about any of those traits while you're this angry."

"What then?"

"Passion. You're a passionate person, Garrett. I've never met someone who goes all in, in quite the same way as you do," she admitted.

"Now, you're just trying to flatter me so I don't take off and teach your professor the right way to speak to a lady," he said.

"You also have a habit of changing the subject any time someone compliments you, which tells me that despite the tough front and sometimes cocky attitude you're actually humble." She stopped there, figuring he would stop her anyway.

"I'm pretty sure you're talking about someone else and I'm about to blush if you keep going, but I'd be honored to buy lunch if you'll allow me to." A smile ghosted his lips despite him trying to let the comments bounce off.

It occurred to her in that moment that he didn't see himself in the same light as she did. It was beyond her how he could *not* know these things about himself. And then, like a ton of bricks, the truth hit her. He didn't know those things because he didn't believe them to be true.

"Deal," she said. Was there a way to help him see himself through her eyes in the short time they would be together? She sure hoped so. It was the least she could do considering how willing he'd been to pitch in and help her.

BRIANNA WAS MISGUIDED. Lack of sleep and too much studying had caused the woman to lose her judgment. Not that he didn't appreciate the compliments. Who wouldn't? But, man, she was so off base there was no guiding her back to the plate.

She seemed to believe what was coming out of her mouth. So his only recourse to change topics was to feed her.

There was a diner near campus he wanted to check out. He'd looked it up on his phone while she'd been in class and the place was highly rated for its home cooking. He could use a real meal about now. Chicken-fried steak with mashed potatoes and gravy would hit the spot.

He also thought about her professor. The man wasn't getting away with using his position to pressure Brianna into doing who knew what. She was strong and knew how to handle advances like that and hearing her say the words had still been a gut punch. What about a younger student? Would she be as strong? Garrett wanted to get back on campus after lunch to do a little investigating. See if anyone else had a bad experience with this prof.

The diner held true to its online reputation of being one of the most popular food stops in the area. The lot brimmed with cars and trucks.

"I've never heard of this place." Brianna's voice held very little of the lightness he remembered from years ago now. She'd always been a spitfire. Something else was missing too that he couldn't quite put his finger on. Happiness?

If only Garrett could say or do something to give that back to her. She had other qualities now. Qualities worth admiring. Strength. Willpower. And there was still just enough sass to remind him she could kick butt when she needed to.

The image of her rejecting the prof from earlier stuck in his mind. She shouldn't have to be so good at defending herself. A lightning bolt struck. Was that the reason she was so good at pushing people away? Pushing him away?

"Let's see if it's worth all the rave." He parked his truck and then hopped out, coming around to the other side as she opened the door for herself and slipped out. She slammed the door a little harder than she had to but he figured it was her way of working out some of the tension she must be feeling.

Setting his own thoughts aside, he reached for her

hand. Instead of pushing him away, she grabbed on tight, linking their fingers as they walked inside the diner.

Eats Diner was a silver tube like a car on a train. The entrance was positioned in the middle of the room and there were an equal number of red vinyl booths to either side. A handwritten sign stood two steps inside the place, asking diners to wait to be seated.

A long bar stretched the length of the space on the opposite wall. Mirrors made the diner look bigger than it was and the smells coming from the kitchen already had his mouth salivating.

A loud growl came from Brianna's stomach, so he figured he'd hit it out of the park with this one and just in time.

"I didn't realize how hungry I was until right now," she said as her cheeks turned a couple shades of red.

"I'm starving." He glanced at his wristwatch. Yes, he still wore one because it wasn't always convenient to take out his phone on a ranch and cell service was always spotty anyway. Much of the time when he was working, he kept his cell in a backpack in his truck or in a sack when he rode his horse. And, yes, he still worked cattle with a horse. A whole lot of ranchers used trucks and ATVs. This was more than a job. It was a way of life. Being on horseback kept him closer to nature. He preferred the sound of hooves to a motor any day of the week and twice on Sunday.

He wasn't kidding either. He was so hungry that he was about to grab a piece of bacon off someone else's plate. Brianna must have read his mind because she gripped his hand even tighter.

"Don't think about it," she warned and at least there was a hint of playfulness in her voice again.

"I wasn't actually going to steal someone else's food," he defended.

"You were thinking about it, though. Weren't you?"

"What makes you think that?" He offered his most innocent look.

"I saw the way you were looking at that guy's plate. And then a little dribble of saliva appeared in the corner of your mouth. Right there." She brought her free hand up to point at his left side.

"Fine. Busted. But I still wasn't going to take anything." He cracked a smile at her observation.

"How many, sweetheart?" A blonde who looked to be in her early thirties bebopped on over as she winked at Garrett. She had on a retro outfit that consisted of neon pink hot pants and a matching shirt with oversize white lapels that looked straight out of the sixties.

"Just the two of us." Brianna held up their linked hands in what he was pretty certain was a show of claiming her territory.

Garrett suppressed a smirk. He and Brianna might not be a thing, but she sure as hell didn't seem to want this waitress flirting with him. To be fair, he was holding Brianna's hand and the wink would qualify as out of line.

The waitress shrugged and said, "This way then."

Brianna stepped in front of Garrett, essentially placing herself in between him and the waitress, and this time he went all in with the charm.

When the blonde stopped in front of a table and turned, Brianna took a step back, which brought her back against his chest. She reached behind her for his hands and wrapped them around her.

The explosion of heat rocketing through him with the move wiped the smile off his face as he tried not to concentrate on the fact that the action caused her sweet round bottom to press into him.

Blood flew south and what he was hungry for shifted. *Not the time nor the place, O'Connor.* Definitely the right woman, though. An image of the two of them tangled in his sheets, heaving for air after a mind-blowing round of sex took center stage.

Since he was no longer a hormonal teenager, he forced his attention back to lunch. *Chicken-fried steak.* All he needed to do was think about chicken-fried steak instead of...

"Here you go." The waitress, whose name tag read Hailey, presented the booth like she was unveiling a new car. The look on her face was priceless as she gave them a once-over. If Brianna was trying to make Hailey jealous, she nailed it.

He couldn't erase the grin on his face after Hailey walked away.

"What was that all about?" he asked Brianna after claiming their seats.

"No idea." She shrugged like it was no big deal.

"Are you ready to talk?" The woman knew how to drive him mad.

"What do you mean? We're talking right now." Confusion knitted her eyebrows together.

"I'm not talking about idle conversation. If I'm going to be of any help to you, you're going to need to let me in."

She stared at him like they were back in middle school and he'd just dared her to kiss Shawn Fletcher. Then, she folded her arms across her chest and said, "Yes."

Chapter Eleven

"What's his name?"

Brianna was certain her face twisted up at the question based on Garrett's response.

"The professor. You never told me his name and…" He stopped long enough for Hailey to turn over two cups and then pour coffee.

At least Hailey didn't wink at Garrett this time like he was some kind of stud in a bar, eager to be hit on. It was gross and stirred a reaction in Brianna. Hailey needed to take a step back and Brianna had done her best to make certain she did. She didn't plan out the actions she'd taken and she had no regrets.

Hailey clearly got the message because when she took out her pad and pen she looked at Brianna this time instead of pretending she wasn't there. Not that Brianna could blame Hailey for wanting to hit on Garrett. The guy was sex-on-a-stick hotness. But Brianna was standing right next to him and they were holding hands. She refused to be ignored.

"What'll it be today?" Hailey asked.

"I'll have chicken-fried steak with mashed potatoes and gravy. Oh, and the fried okra. Is it any good?" Brianna handed over the menu in time to watch Hailey's eyes light up.

"Ours is the best. I know everyone says that but I'm telling you right now that no one compares to ours." Hailey's demeanor changed. So much so, Brianna was sold.

"Then, I have to try those," she said.

"And you, sir?" Hailey's voice held a whole lot more respect now.

"I'll have the exact same." He handed over his menu and then Hailey scurried away with a smile. He focused on Brianna and his gaze caused her cheeks to burn. "Nice touch, by the way."

"What?" She played like she didn't know what he was talking about.

"I saw what you did there."

"It was nothing." She waved her hand like she was dismissing the idea.

"It was great," was all he said before shaking his head with a slight smile that made her heart free-fall. His chest was puffed out just a little, enough to make her think he was proud of her.

A surprising tear welled up. She coughed and tucked her chin to her chest so she could gain hold of her emotions before looking up at Garrett again.

"I can always figure it out on my own," Garrett's voice broke through the moment. "I'd rather you be the one to tell me."

"What are you going to do to him?" She pulled it together enough to risk a glance at him.

"Nothing until you tell me I can." The tension in his eyes returned and she stared in the face of anger.

"You'll never know how much it means to me that you care…but I need to fight my own battles," she said.

Her words seemed to resonate. After a few seconds, he looked away before taking a sip of coffee.

"Any chance you'd be willing to let me back you up or at the very least be around to watch it happen? I have a feeling you're going to tan his hide when you get around to it," he said with that smirk she was beginning to love.

Whoa, there. Slow down. Love was a strong word. *Like* was better. And she very much liked to see that mischief in his eyes.

"Deal," she said by way of response.

Before they could shake on it, plates arrived. The smell of the chicken-fried steak didn't do justice to how amazing it looked. The batter was caramel colored and crisp. If this dish tasted half as good as it looked, her taste buds were in for a treat. She'd deal with her thighs later. Or not. Running around behind a bar all night kept her in decent enough shape. A few curves didn't bother her.

Hailey's expression was priceless after she set the plates in front of them and scanned their faces. "Y'all go on and enjoy. Holler if you need anything else."

She slid the bill onto the table with a slight curtsy.

"We sure will," Brianna said. She'd served enough couples to realize when a man and woman walked into a bar or anywhere else for that matter together, the server's attention should be on the woman. It was basic etiquette in the service industry. Hailey had taken the hint, though. Her service was better for it too.

"Dr. Jenkins is his name, by the way," she said to Garrett as she picked up her knife and fork.

Not many other sounds were made until the plates were clean other than the occasional moan from sheer pleasure.

"How did I not know about this place? It's so close to campus," Brianna said when she was so full she thought she might burst. A glance at the bill told her why. The eatery was proud of their dishes and placed value on them. And the food was worth every cent.

She promised she'd come back here after graduation. Speaking of which, she needed to think about the next step of getting a few interviews lined up. She had no plans to stick around the bar a day longer than she had to.

"It was hyped on the internet and I wasn't so sure it would live up." He picked up his coffee and drained his second cup. "Call me a satisfied customer."

"I could use a nap," she said as an image of her curled up in bed with Garrett assaulted her. She shoved it aside, thinking she needed to keep her mind far away from that temptation. She caught his gaze. "Thank you. For helping me last night despite the fact I must've looked like a drowned rat to you. And for this today."

He waved her away like it was nothing. It wasn't. In fact, it was everything to her. She couldn't remember the last time someone volunteered to show up for her like this.

"I know you have a life and—"

His hand came up again to wave her off. "It's nothing you wouldn't do for me if the situation was reversed."

"Why are you so confident about that?" She could tell he was too. There wasn't a hint of doubt in his eyes—eyes that she could stare into all day.

"Because I know you. You might have grown up and so have I. But you're still the same underneath it all and we were close once even though it hurt my relationship with my brother at the time," he admitted.

"I'm sorry about that. I always felt bad about it." The thought she'd been the one to drive a wedge between brothers hit her square in the chest.

"You couldn't have if Colton and I had been closer," he said without hesitation. "We always had a competitive relationship. I can't even remember how it began or what started it, to be honest. Must have been something when we were kids. Of all the boys, we fought the most. We were the most competitive."

"Then, you must be the most alike deep down," she said.

He stopped for a second and considered her statement. "I'm not sure I follow."

"Think about it. What happens when you put two roosters in a henhouse?" It was the best analogy she could think up on a stomach so full she was afraid the top button of her pants would pop.

"It gets ugly," he conceded.

"Exactly. Two alpha males in close proximity fight. Happens in nature all the time," she said.

"Yeah, but it happened to the two of us. My other brothers are strong-willed, but I don't fight with them."

"Then, you and Colton must possess a quality the other doesn't like in himself. I would definitely say the two of you are more alike when it comes to personality than any of the others," she stated.

"Really?" The news seemed to shock him.

"I think so," she admitted.

All he said was, "Huh."

"Oh, man. I ate way too much." Brianna bit back a yawn.

"Good. Where we're going you'll be able to walk it off."

GARRETT'S CELL BUZZED as he walked out of the restaurant. He almost ignored it, figuring it was one of his brothers, but decided to check anyway. Colton's ears were probably burning and that was the reason for the call. He checked the screen and froze. Damiani. Garrett needed to take this one.

"Hey, can you hold on a sec?" he asked.

"Not too long. I got something hot." Damiani's full name was Anthony DeLuca Damiani but he only responded to his last name. He was a private detective.

"No problem." Garrett fished out his truck keys and tossed them to Brianna, who'd taken a couple of steps toward the vehicle. "You go ahead. I'll be right there."

She caught the keys and then cocked her head to one side. "Okay."

He winked at her before returning to the call.

"Hey, man. What did you find?" Damiani was a New York transplant who'd moved to Austin to set up a private investigations shop. He and Garrett dated sisters a couple of years ago. The relationships didn't work out but Damiani and Garrett kept in touch, went out for a beer whenever Garrett was in town.

"There's an alpaca farm that gives tours during the day but also is believed to be a front for a baby ring. I got the San Antonio tip wrong," he hedged. "It wasn't his credit card."

"I know you did." Garrett wasn't trying to make his buddy feel bad about it. "But, seriously, alpacas?"

"Yeah. I know. It's kind of brilliant when you really think about it. Farmland gets a government blessing, and who would think anything sinister was happening there?" Damiani said.

"And why do you think there's something fishy going on?" Garrett asked.

"A tip. I'd rather not say who it came from. I was doing a little fishing of my own and got lucky," he said.

In Garrett's experience, luck happened more often to someone working hard to find answers.

"That's not the tip, though," Damiani said.

"What is?" Garrett asked.

"My guy says someone named Finn O'Connor was asking around about the place." Damiani's voice lowered when he said, "Again, I'd like to express my condolences. I didn't know your father personally, but he sounds like a straight-up guy, you know."

"Yeah. I appreciate it." Garrett needed a second to process what he was hearing, or more important, to steel himself for what he was about to learn. "Where is this place and what's it called?"

"It's off I-35 about a mile north of Killeen," Damiani said before rattling off the address. "Alpaca Rescue is the name of the place. They're a nonprofit but word on the street is that they make their money on what happens inside the house, not so much as in the barn, if you know what I mean."

Killeen was about halfway between Austin and Waco. In no traffic, Waco wasn't much more than a two-hour drive but there was almost always traffic. Tack on another hour to San Antonio. All in all, about five hours round trip under the best circumstances. The loop around Austin was a lifesaver even though it added a couple of miles. Not having to stop every five seconds or move at a crawl was worth any price.

"I respect that you can't give me a name, but I need to know how reliable this source is." If this was true—and he had no reason to doubt Damiani— someone was willing to kill to keep a secret.

"On a scale of one to ten...he's a twelve." Damiani's voice dropped when he said, "Hey, be careful with this one. You know what I mean? I've got like two friends I actually enjoy meeting up with for a beer and you're one of 'em."

"Thanks, man. I feel the same." Garrett was sincere. He knew a lot of people and called very few of them friends.

"You'll be the first to know should I hear anything else," Damiani said. "In the meantime, watch your back."

"I'll be around for that beer real soon," Garrett said for good measure.

"I'll save you a seat at Dublin's on Sixth."

Garrett thanked Damiani before ending the call and heading toward the truck. He climbed in the driver's seat. "That was news about my dad's case."

He filled her in as he started the engine.

"Listen, Garrett. I totally understand if you need to bail. Your dad's case is way more important and I don't want to keep you any longer than—"

"I'm here. I'm seeing this thing through with you just like I said I would. Believe me, I'd feel a helluva lot worse if I took off to follow up on a lead—and that's all it is at this point—and something happened to you," he admitted. "Plus, there's nothing I can do to bring my dad back at this point."

She was chewing the inside of her cheek, her tell that she was uncomfortable about something. It used to signal she hadn't studied for a test like she believed she should have back in school. He took it as a sign she needed a bit more convincing.

"Besides, I might be able to slip out in the morning while you're asleep and make a run. If I go early enough, I should be able to round trip before…" He stopped right there. "What time is your class tomorrow?"

"Same as this morning but it's an hour and a half," she said. She immediately went back to working the inside of her cheek.

A quick calculation said there was no way he would be back in time. Using his smartphone, he pulled up the internet and searched for the Alpaca Rescue. Much to his surprise, several rescue organizations came up. He had no idea the alpaca population was at risk to this degree. He chalked it up to people getting excited about a pet or even starting a small operation for the fur before realizing how much work it was.

The same thing happened in ranching. Folks got stars in their eyes about living on the open range in an old farmhouse. They pictured the sunsets, which were spectacular. They envisioned having all the fun that came with an animal, which made the work worth it. They got caught up in the romance of it without realizing how hard the day-to-day care could be. First of all, there was a lot of manual labor in a trade like cattle ranching even with machines to make it all easier now.

Most newcomers didn't get past the first year before they were ready to pack up and head back to where they came. Disease could wipe out a herd. Then there were all the financial considerations. Plenty of ranches weren't profitable and if they were, they eked by.

Finn O'Connor had been a pioneer in the industry. He was the first to ensure herds were grass fed and fetched a higher price for organics.

Most folks jumped into owning a ranch with both feet, never doing all the research upfront. He likened the experience to rehabbing an old house. They were called money pits for a reason.

Brianna was quiet on the way back to campus. Garrett didn't say much either but that didn't mean the wheels weren't spinning in his head. He didn't want to wait too long to check into the alpaca situation. It might be nothing, but it might just crack open the whole case and they'd been waiting too long for answers already. An itch of excitement took hold as he thought about the possibility of finding out who killed his father and what had happened to his sister. What if it was more bad news?

His chest squeezed thinking about the day he would be able to tell his mother what happened to Caroline. Even bad news was better than not knowing.

The next question was whether or not he should bring in his brothers. Too early, he thought. It would be best to wait on it and see if the lead panned out. No one missed him at the ranch. No one expected him to be home. Each of his brothers had reached out recently, some letting him know exactly what they thought about his absence.

But what if he did go home? Then what? Would he get comfortable? Give up the search? Settle?

Did he believe most of his brothers had done the same thing? In truth, Garrett hadn't given it a whole lot of thought. In fact, he'd been so focused on shaming himself for not cracking the case that he didn't really think a whole lot about the others. He hadn't talked to them about it much either. He knew several of his brothers used their jobs to poke around when they could. They had protocols to abide by and oaths to follow.

That was the great thing about Garrett's life. He answered to no one except himself. If he needed to break a law to find out the truth, so be it. He would never hurt an innocent person to get what he wanted, though.

But had he really done all that he could have? The voice in the back of his head chimed in with a resounding *no*. Too often, he'd fallen into the cycle of heading nowhere and then becoming so frustrated that he had to spend some time on the land to rebalance himself. Anger kept him away from people for weeks when he could have pivoted and found a new lead. He'd go off and do something stupid and then the cycle of shame would start over again. He'd condemn his own stupidity and it all spiraled from there.

Recognizing the pattern was all well and good except that he didn't know how to break it. So lotta good it did. Once the cycle started, it was like watching a Mack truck come right at him with no ability to step out of its way.

"Garrett?" The concern in Brianna's voice shocked him out of his revelry.

"Yeah?"

"Are you going to get out of the truck or are we going to sit here all day?" she asked. "Also, you didn't tell me why we came back here."

He looked around, and realized he'd parked in the same spot as earlier at her school.

"Right. I think I know how to find out how to get information about the creep who dropped out of your class."

"Really?" She sounded a little more than shocked.

"It was either this or hack into the mainframe," he teased, trying to lighten the heavy mood that had descended on him. He was certain she'd picked up on it too. "Come on, I'm kidding. I barely know how to work my phone. I'm the last person who would have the skills to break into a computer."

She forced a laugh. At least, it sounded forced anyway. And the smile she gave didn't reach her eyes. Concern, however, was abundant in the tension lines in her face.

"Trust me?" he asked, hoping he'd gained a little of her confidence in the past eighteen or so hours.

"I'm willing to go out on a limb."

They were making progress. Pride shouldn't swell in his chest. It did, though.

"Have you ever thought about having kids?" Brianna asked out of the blue.

"Where'd that question come from?" He didn't bother to mask the shock in his voice. To say she'd caught him off guard was a lot like saying milk came from cows.

"Curious, I guess." She shrugged but he wasn't buying it.

It dawned on him she must be referring to what happened to his sister. He thought about it for a long moment before answering. Not because he didn't know the answer to the question but because he'd never opened up to anyone before about something so personal.

For reasons he couldn't explain and sure as hell didn't want to examine, he decided to go for it.

"To answer your question…yes, I have thought about whether or not I wanted to have kids," he said. "The second part of that answer is a hard no."

The fact she didn't seem surprised or upset shouldn't bother him. So, why did it?

Chapter Twelve

Brianna walked behind Garrett as they entered the Administration Building, thinking about how he'd hesitated before answering her question in the parking lot. She didn't blame him for not wanting kids after what his family had been through. Forget that he wasn't even born yet when the kidnapping had occurred. She couldn't imagine a parent ever truly getting over the loss of a child. Not knowing what happened had to be even worse. Always having a question mark hanging over their heads. Never getting answers. Her heart ached for the O'Connor family and their loss. There were no words to ease that brand of pain.

"Am I too late to drop a class?" Garrett's question seemed to throw the office aide off.

Her face scrunched. "I'm sorry. You'll have to get your prof's permission at this point."

The young brunette in a high ponytail with cheekbones most any woman would kill for scooted her chair to the desk where Brianna stood behind Garrett. From her vantage point, she could see the young adult blushing under Garrett's stare.

The guy could work magic on pretty much any woman he wanted. Probably men too with his good looks, she mused.

"And what if he doesn't give it to me?" Garrett continued in that smooth-as-silk voice Brianna was certain was meant to butter the brunette up. So, he wasn't against using his considerable charms to get the information they needed. Maybe the lead he got in his father's case had him wanting to speed hers up so he could move on.

As much as she wanted…*needed*…to bust the creep who was freaking her out every few nights on her rides home from work, the thought of Garrett taking off and her old life returning was a gut punch she wasn't expecting.

That *was* the deal. He was kind enough to stick around until the creep either got spooked by his presence and bolted or was locked behind bars where he belonged. She reminded herself that was enough no matter how much her heart protested. If she listened to it, she would be living on a ranch somewhere with this man while chasing after a kiddo or two.

Oh, no. Where did that little news bulletin come from?

Since she didn't want to block any of his mojo, she stayed tucked behind him. His hand occasionally reached back to touch her…reassure her? Any time their skin came in contact a trill of awareness rippled through her. Did he have to be so dang sexy? And caring?

Seriously, though, ever since the call at the diner his demeanor had changed. She had to figure out a way to convince him not to wait to follow up on the lead. What if he waited and the lead dried up? Would he always blame her?

Even if he didn't, she would. She would never forgive herself if he let something slide as important as finding out what happened to his sister or locking behind bars the person who killed his father. Finn O'Connor had been truly one of the most decent and kindest people on earth. Whenever she heard the term *salt-of-the-earth*, she thought of him. He'd welcomed her on the ranch along with anyone else his sons brought home. He worked side by side with his ranch hands and foreman. As far as she could tell, he never took the easy road over doing what was right.

Tears welled in her eyes thinking about his life being cut short. His wife was just as decent and kind as he was. She certainly didn't deserve to lose the love of her life. Losing a daughter, her firstborn, was more than anyone should have to endure. And yet, she'd found a way to keep going despite what had to be a parent's worst nightmare. Brianna hadn't given much thought to having children of her own until the idea popped into her thoughts a few seconds ago. She figured there was plenty of time for that later if she wanted a family, and that was a big *if.* There was no way she could think about kids when she was struggling to take care of herself.

But she was beginning to realize nothing was guaranteed, and later might turn into not at all without her consent. Plus, she never really bought into the whole happily-ever-after lie. People met and fell in love all the time. And then plenty of them fell out of love or, worse yet, fell in love with someone else while they were still married. She could attest to the level of pain that caused.

Her hand instinctively came up to the charm on her necklace. She fingered the lucky piece as more tears welled in her eyes. Refusing to give in to the emotion threatening to suck her under, she glanced around in hopes of finding something else to focus on.

To her left, one of her classmates, who appeared to be working in the office, caught her eye. Oh, what was her name?

Lauren Bishop. She sat next to Brianna most of the time in class and Brianna had seen the name scribbled down on the attendance sign-up sheet enough times for it to stick.

She didn't realize Lauren worked here. Then again, it wasn't like Brianna was in school to make friends. Lauren stood out. One, because she sat next to Brianna most of the time. Two, because she had a string of beads on her backpack that looked like a little kid's preschool art project.

Maybe Brianna could do a little digging of her own. She walked over to Lauren, leaving Garrett to his conversation.

"Hey, Lauren," Brianna said like the two of them were besties rather than two strangers who sat next to each other in class and gave the occasional nod or smile during lectures.

Lauren looked up from the screen she was studying and returned the smile. "Hi. Can I help you?"

Based on the way her left eyebrow arched ever so slightly and her gaze fixed on Brianna, Lauren was trying to place where she knew Brianna from.

Rather than give herself away, Brianna decided to run with it. "I didn't realize you worked in the office."

"Work-study," Lauren corrected. "It's part of my financial aid."

"Oh, nice," Brianna said a little too cheerfully based on Lauren's slight frown. "I'm sure it helps pay the bills."

"It covers my sitter," Lauren said.

"Little girl or little boy?" Brianna might not know much about kids but she knew how to get people talking from her experience as a bartender. Most people couldn't wait to talk about themselves.

"Girl." Lauren studied Brianna for a long moment. "Do you have kids?"

Brianna excelled at building rapport with her clients and that meant finding common ground. If she was going to do the same with Lauren, she would have to find a different topic.

"Not yet," Brianna said. It wasn't exactly a lie. She didn't have kids *yet*. This wasn't the time or place to go into detail about how she never wanted them either. But then that wasn't exactly true. She'd had a fleeting thought about having Garrett's babies.

"Believe me when I tell you that it's better to wait

until you finish school." Lauren gave Brianna a quick once-over and she assumed the woman was trying to figure out an age.

"I hear you," Brianna said, hoping this would lead to the perfect opportunity to get Lauren talking about class. "But now I'm in a spot because…"

She paused mainly for dramatic effect. If Lauren thought she was teasing information out of Brianna she'd be more invested, and that meant more likely to help.

"Never mind. It's nothing." Brianna waved a hand like she was swatting a fly.

"What?" Lauren scooted her chair away from the monitor and toward Brianna. "Go ahead. You can tell me." She glanced around. "Who am I going to tell anyway?"

"Well… I don't know," Brianna hedged.

"It's fine." Lauren leaned over the desk.

"Okay, but it's not really a big deal. I'll figure it out…"

"Figure what out?" Lauren asked.

"A guy from class. We're supposed to partner on a project and he's not here. He gave me his cell number but I can't read his handwriting. Anyway, I can't afford to fail the class. You know? Not with graduation around the corner. I'm so close and so tired of working nights to pay for school." Brianna threw in the last bit for good measure. It was truer than she wanted it to be and about as honest as she'd ever been. The cell phone bit was stretching the truth and she hated doing it. It didn't feel good to deceive someone, but Lauren's fingers were already busy dancing across the keyboard.

"I know the guy you're talking about." Her forehead creased. "Thought he'd been assigned to another group, though."

Brianna wasn't sure what would come up on Lauren's screen. She'd found out the hard way the computer systems at her school did a lousy job of talking to each other. She could only hope Lauren wouldn't see that Derk had dropped the class. Possibly dropped out of school. If the latter was true, Brianna was about to be busted.

Maybe not, she reasoned. She could always say she didn't realize he'd chunked the whole semester.

Her pulse climbed another notch with every second Lauren stared at the screen.

"Got it." Lauren practically beamed. She glanced up and gave Brianna a once-over. "Ready?"

"Yeah." Brianna fumbled for her cell. "This is great. I can't thank you enough. This will be such a huge help."

"I know what it's like to have a partner ditch. Believe me when I say it's no fun. Not everyone here is as focused as some of us." She gave a look of solidarity.

"Right. I got a C on a group project because the person who did all of the graphics decided to stop coming to class," Brianna shared as she palmed her cell. She held it up into the air. "Ready when you are."

Lauren rattled off the number. Then, she leaned over the desk. "Just don't tell anyone it came from me.

I can't afford to lose my financial aid." She reached under her desk and pulled out a cell phone. "This is Landy."

The toothless grin on the round-faced angel in the picture tugged at Brianna's heart. Her ovaries cried.

"Your daughter is beautiful." Brianna had never meant those words more. Her chest squeezed at the thought she could end up getting Lauren in trouble or cost that little girl stability. "And I won't tell a soul about this." She held up her cell and used it to cross her heart.

Lauren's eyes widened and her cheeks turned six shades past red. Her gaze fixed on something moving behind Brianna. Or should she say *someone*?

"Are you ready?" Garrett's chest pressed to her back as he said those words in her ear. His warm breath sent a trill of awareness skittering down the delicate skin at the nape of her neck. An image of their babies popped into Brianna's thoughts, a boy who was the spitting image of his father and a little girl who resembled Brianna. Talk about ovaries crying and her heart melting.

How much trouble was she in right now? A helluva lot more than she wanted to acknowledge.

GARRETT FIGURED BRIANNA needed an out. He gave her one. Pretending to be *together* had been as natural as waking in the morning. So, why didn't he want to get out of bed?

Figuratively, of course. But then, literally didn't sound so bad to him right now either.

All that talk about babies earlier should have sleeping with Brianna at the bottom of his list. He suppressed a smile. There wasn't much that could manage that feat.

Brianna cleared her throat. "Yeah. I'm ready when you are."

He reached for her hand and then linked their fingers.

"See you in class," Brianna said to the person she'd been talking to. He'd realized the second she'd disappeared from behind him earlier. Keeping her in his peripheral, he saw her talking to an employee.

"On Thursday." The worker broke off her stare before moving to the monitor and refocusing her attention there.

"Who was that?" he asked as soon as they stepped outside.

"Someone from class," Brianna said. "How'd you do, by the way?"

"Struck out," he admitted.

"Well then I'm glad I saw my classmate." She practically beamed.

"What did you get?"

"A cell phone number," she said. "Which will allow us to do a reverse phone lookup."

He was familiar with a website that offered the service for a small fee. "We can get his address if we're lucky."

"That's right," she said.

"Do I want to know why you know about this?" he asked.

"Probably not," she hedged. "Nothing illegal, if that's what you're wondering."

"Nope. I didn't figure you for the type to break the law," he said.

"Before you nominate me for sainthood, you should know that I fudged the truth back there. I feel terrible about it too." Her shoulders drooped with the admission.

Her honesty was one of her many admirable traits.

"Don't be too hard on yourself, Bri." He caught himself right there. The term of endearment had no place in their relationship. He used to call her that when they were a couple. "Look, Brianna, you're trying to save your life. This isn't a game. If you had to stretch the truth to get information, it's what you had to do. Doesn't make you a bad person."

"No?" There was a look of hurt in her eyes when she caught his gaze again. She dropped his hand and picked up the pace toward his truck.

He wasn't quite ready to leave yet but by the looks of her, she was done with campus for the day. A question loomed like a heavy cloud. Why did the air between them suddenly turn so cold? He was trying to give her an out, reassure her that she wasn't the worst possible person on the planet like she was trying to convince herself. How had his plan backfired?

"What did I do, Brianna? What did I say that was so wrong?" he asked.

Her hand was on the door handle of the passenger side by the time he caught up to her.

"Seriously. Tell me because I have no idea and the last thing I want to do is hurt you," he said.

She froze for a solid minute before inhaling slowly like she was breathing for the first time.

Gradually, she turned around and then leaned against the truck, eyes closed. She brought her hands up to her temples. "It's what she used to say. The part about lying not making you a bad person."

"She? Who?" And then it dawned on him. "Your mother?"

"Yes." A lone tear streaked her cheek as she dropped one hand down to her side and the other to her chest.

As he approached, he saw that she was fingering the charm on the necklace she wore.

"Nothing was ever anyone's fault with her. But she hurt everyone in her wake." More of those tears streamed down her cheeks.

He reached up and thumbed them away.

"I'm sorry," he said, low and under his breath. "I had no idea."

"It's not your fault," she hurriedly countered. She was too quick to let others off the hook.

"No. It is my fault. I should have known," he argued.

"How would you?" She blinked her eyes open—pure, beautiful eyes that were like looking into a window to her soul. Eyes that held more hurt than any one person should have to bear.

Before debating his next actions, he closed the distance between them, brought his hand up around the base of her neck and pulled her toward him as he brought his lips to hers. Before they touched, he said, "I'm sorry."

She put her hands up against his chest, fists he half expected to pound against him. They didn't. She didn't. Instead, she grabbed fistfuls of his shirt and tugged him closer.

When his mouth touched hers, a thousand fireworks went off inside his chest. He could only imagine how incredible sex with Brianna would be based on the heat in the few kisses they'd shared.

She moaned against his lips, the sweetest, sexiest sound he'd ever heard. Claiming her mouth as his, he dipped his tongue inside those full lips of hers. Honeysuckle never tasted so sweet.

His pulse went from zero to sixty in two seconds flat when she dug her hands into his shirt even more. Her breath was coming out in gasps as tension built inside him, seeking an outlet.

She was the only one who could give him the sweet release he craved.

"Garrett," she moaned against his lips. Hearing his name roll off her tongue was about the most alluring sound. More blood flew south as his own desire mounted.

A stray thought struck that he should probably tone this down in the campus parking lot, but he wasn't about to listen to it. Couldn't even if he tried. Not while those cherry lips of hers moved against his. She bit down on his bottom lip and scraped her teeth across it as she released, and he realized he couldn't let this continue unchecked. Not if he was going to keep his vow to walk away once this was over. And he had every intention of doing just that despite the ache already forming in his chest at the thought.

Much to his surprise, Brianna was the one who pulled back first.

Chapter Thirteen

"We can't do this." Brianna repeated the statement more for her own benefit than Garrett's as her breath came out in gasps. It was true no matter how they looked at it or who was the first to stop. She'd felt the tension in his lips when he had the same thought as she did.

She brought the back of her hand up to her lips, tried to steady her breathing. There was some small measure of satisfaction in the fact he was breathing as hard as she was. In fact, it caused her to crack a smile.

Garrett took one look at her and his face broke into a wide smile, as well. "I know and yet you have no idea how much willpower it's taking right now not to lean forward and claim that beautiful mouth of yours."

"Now I have it on record," she teased.

His dark brow arched.

"You think I'm beautiful," she quipped with a self-satisfied smirk.

"I have no plans to take it back." He referred to the way they used to tease each other years ago.

Brianna laughed, the full-belly kind. She couldn't remember the last time she'd done that, so she didn't fight it. She let laughter roll up and out until her stomach hurt and her cheeks burned from smiling so much.

Gorgeous Garrett O'Connor stood there, one arm resting on his truck, laughing right along with her.

The moment was cut short when a blue hatchback crept by two aisles over. The brakes squeaked and she couldn't shake the feeling that the car's driver was looking for something other than a parking spot. The whole scene was odd enough to remind her they were standing out in broad daylight.

Without a word, they hopped into action. Garrett opened the truck door for her and she immediately thanked him and climbed inside. He quickly closed the door and claimed the driver's seat. Within a minute, they were navigating toward the blue hatchback. Or, at least where it had been. Classes must have been changing because the parking lot was suddenly like an ant farm with cars coming and going, and people flooding the lot.

The hatchback was gone by the time they got to his aisle. Garrett rolled the windows down, no doubt listening for the sound of the brakes to no avail.

Conversation on the ride back to her place was dampened but lighter than it had been.

"I'll be honest with you, Garrett. I can't remember the last time I laughed as hard as we did back there," she finally said as he pulled into a visitor's spot at her apartment.

"If I'm perfectly honest, same here." He leaned his head back on his head rest. "We should laugh more, shouldn't we?"

It was more statement than question.

"Why don't we?" she asked.

"Maybe another question is when did life get so serious?"

She couldn't agree more there. Based on the way his shoulders slumped and he closed his eyes, she figured he felt that statement in every part of his body.

"Bills started coming due, I guess." She'd had her electricity cut off twice when she was first starting out on her own. Sleeping on a coworker's couch wasn't exactly her idea of fun. Neither was fighting off his drunk roommate when he came home to find her there alone. "But you were always more…"

She stopped right there not wanting to ruin the mood by hurting his feelings.

"Go on," he urged anyway, straightening his neck before turning to look at her. "Say it."

"Nah—"

"You can't stop in the middle of a sentence. What would Mrs. Dooley think?" He'd lightened his voice but there was still a serious undertone.

"Our English teacher probably doesn't care what happened to us," she admitted. They weren't exactly popular with teachers. Well, she took that back. Most O'Connors were, just not Garrett. But he always seemed to go out of his way to separate himself from his brothers.

"Then, finish it for my sake," he countered.

"*You* are the reason I decided to hold my tongue," she said.

"Pretend I'm someone else and come out with it." He was practically begging now. "Never mind."

That sure was a tail whip.

"I thought you wanted to know," she said.

"You're too chicken to say it to my face." Now he really was dragging them back to middle school. She couldn't count the number of times one of them had pulled that line on the other one.

It made her smile.

"All right, but you have to promise not to get mad. Or think I don't appreciate everything you're doing for me." She shot a warning look.

He brought both in a truce.

"Intense. I was going to say that you've always been intense. There. Are you happy now?" she asked, trying to keep the mood light.

"Yes. I kind of am." He laughed out loud.

"It's true. You always had a chip on your shoulder. You know? Like you didn't think you belonged in the O'Connor family or something," she said.

"It's hard to live up to my brothers," he admitted. The hurt returned to his eyes and she hated that she was the one who caused it. "I think I decided early on the only way to stand out in a family like mine was to cause trouble."

"You were never all that bad, Garrett. Just intense, like I said."

"Yeah, that's like the third time you've used that word in the past minute," he mused.

"Sorry. I don't mean it in a bad way. When you set your sights on something, you used that focus for good," she pointed out.

"Most of the time, I've been using it to mess up my life royally," he said.

She caught his gaze and held it. "It's never too late to change, Garrett. Look at me. I'm claiming my future."

"A future that doesn't make you so excited that you're ready to jump out of bed every morning," he said. Again, his hands went up. "I'm not trying to be a jerk here. I'm just trying to better understand what makes you tick."

"My future might not be exciting, but neither is having your electricity cut off because you couldn't pay the bill or living in a cramped apartment for the rest of your life," she said plain as the nose on her face. With Garrett, she didn't feel the need to candy coat her life or what she was trying to do. He'd see right through her if she tried to lie anyway.

"Fair enough." He paused like he was about to say something. Then came, "Ready to go inside and look up that phone number?"

"Yes," she said quickly. A little too quickly?

"How much do you want to bet Derk drives a blue hatchback?" Garrett asked after opening the door for her.

"Wouldn't be against the law if he did." She figured Garrett was on point with that assumption.

"No, it wouldn't."

"Plus, he could be on campus for a whole lot of

other reasons," she said. "And remember, the jerk playing bumper cars with me had a truck."

"True again," he said. "And yet…"

"I know. I agree with you. I'm just pointing out what a cop would tell us. Believe me, I have more experience than I ever wanted with local law enforcement." In fact, if she never saw another officer for the rest of her life she'd be thrilled. They were decent enough and she didn't have anything personal against them. Each one had taken down all the facts of her complaints. They seemed interested in hearing all the details. The net result was the same. There wasn't anything they could do about someone trying to run her off the road. Despite a crime being committed against her, she didn't have a license plate or description of the vehicle or perp. There wasn't much they could do.

If she could figure out who was behind the threat, she could file a restraining order. But she was short on proof. So, each one thanked her and then sent her on her way. The only reason she kept on filing reports was so there would be a history if something bad happened to her and they actually caught the guy. Or, if something happened to her and they needed to look for someone. She figured one small detail might blow the case wide open.

Which reminded her…

"You're forgetting one small fact," she said to Garrett as she opened the door to her apartment.

"Oh, yeah? What's that?" He followed her inside

and locked the door behind them. His eyebrows drew together in confusion.

"A large vehicle tried to run me off the road. A small hatchback wouldn't be any match against Code Blue," she said. "And I would have remembered a hatchback."

"Code Blue?" He quirked a brow.

"My Jeep," she said.

He cocked his head to one side. "Good point."

GARRETT SUPPRESSED A LAUGH. Code Blue? As far as vehicle names went, that was right up there with the best of 'em. He remembered smiling when he saw the name on her spare tire cover. The annoying-as-all-get-out voice in the back of his head picked that moment to point out that he hadn't laughed this much in one day in forever. Maybe ever.

Brianna had pinned him correctly when she'd called him intense. Hell, did she think he wanted to be this frustrated all the time? Frustrated with his brothers. Frustrated with himself. Frustrated with the world.

When he thought about it in those terms, it sure seemed like a waste of good energy. He still had a couple of axes to grind, but when Brianna's stalker, his sister's kidnapper and his father's killer were locked up where they belonged, he vowed to figure out a way to laugh more.

He needed more levity in his life because in the few moments he'd experienced it with Brianna, he'd been the happiest he could remember.

Figuring out how to be less intense was the hard part. He could start with knocking the chip off his shoulder when it came to his brother Colton.

Brianna pulled her laptop from her backpack and plugged in the power cord. As far as jalopies went, this computer was a doozie. Would she let him buy her something with a little more zip?

"When is your graduation?" he asked before he could stop himself. It was none of his business because he didn't plan on sticking around once they figured out who the jerk was trying to run her off the road. More of that familiar tension knotted in his shoulder blades.

"Um, thirty-six days," she said. She didn't glance up from the screen that was still loading.

Would she accept a new laptop as a graduation gift? He wanted her to start her new career with something nice. Hell, he could always mail one to her. Buy it off the internet and have it shipped. He made a mental note of her address.

On second thought, he didn't want to insult her. She'd been handling life on her terms and, contrary to her belief, handling it well. Better than well. She was amazing. In fact, she was just the type of person he could see himself settling down for the long haul with if he was the "settling down" type. He wasn't and had no intention of changing his ways. It was enough that he'd decided to work on being less intense. There was no need to go overhauling all of his life.

Besides, hadn't he read something about being careful not to make rash decisions while grieving?

And he was grieving. Brianna's case was a distraction. One he needed about now. Because thinking about everything he'd missed out on and would miss out on with his dad for as long as Garrett lived docked a boulder on his chest that made breathing hurt.

Thinking of his dad usually triggered a flight impulse, a need to move on. From painful memories, from sorrow. It was a sentiment he knew well, the desire to be outside, on the go. Being confined in a small space usually made him stir crazy as all get out. But here he was, contented to be in this tiny apartment, not feeling as if he wanted to be anywhere else on earth. He registered the sensation as strange and then tucked it down deep. "Here we go," Brianna said. She turned the screen toward him.

"How far away is that address?" he asked, figuring they needed to get on the road.

"It's close to campus actually. Not too far from where we had lunch, which still makes me want to cry for how good it was," she said.

"We can make the trek back if we—"

"I have to get ready for work. I barely have enough time to pack dinner after driving back and forth to campus." She glanced at the clock on the wall.

"But it's only four-thirty," he said.

"I have twenty minutes to get cleaned up and cram my body into that uniform." She made air quotes with her fingers on the last word. "And then I have to get on the road."

"How far away is the bar?"

"Forty minutes," she said.

"That's a haul," he noted.

"Yep. Exactly. The last thing I wanted was to run into someone from class or, worse yet, one of my professors while tending bar." She involuntarily shuddered.

"Why is that? I mean, wouldn't they come out for the worse in that situation? They are, in fact, the patrons of a bar," he pointed out.

"True. But, I like to keep my worlds separate. At school, I'm a student just like everybody else." She stood. "Right now, I have another 'hat' to wear. Barkeep."

He nodded as she left the room, heading into her adjacent bedroom. He thought back to what had happened with her mother, the affair she'd had with one of the town's prominent men and how that tainted their family name to the point they'd moved to outrun the bad reputation. Brianna's strategy from earlier clicked in his mind and he understood why she would want to be normal after the shame that followed their family.

His chest squeezed remembering the day she'd found him and told him the news her family was moving away. Even though they'd broken up, he'd been crushed. Back then, he'd been head over heels for her. Still was?

But Colton had been too and Garrett hadn't wanted to stand in between the two of them if his brother had had a chance with Brianna.

Did he regret his choice? Considering hindsight was twenty-twenty, the short answer was yes.

Chapter Fourteen

Brianna walked out of the bedroom all done up in her bartending gear and Garrett's heart detonated. He coughed to ease his dry throat, but it did little to help.

"You're beautiful," he managed to say.

She froze, and then caught his gaze. Something stirred in her eyes—an emotion he couldn't quite pinpoint—and the knot in his gut tightened a few more notches. He meant it. She was beautiful. She could be dressed in a potato sack and she would still stun.

There was so much more to her beauty than physical attraction, although she had that in spades. Her intelligence, sharp mind and sense of humor made her darn near irresistible. He almost laughed out loud at that. He was having one helluva time resisting his attraction to her.

"Thank you." The words came out quiet and unsure.

Garrett was floored that she didn't see in herself what was so easy for others to notice. Considering he was having a difficult enough time keeping his thoughts from going down that road again, a road that would be nothing more than a dead end, he decided this wasn't the time for him to convince her.

"Ready?" he asked instead.

"I'll just grab my backpack." She walked past him and her unique citrus-and-fresh-flower scent filled his senses. There was no way he could stand there and allow that to happen so he pushed off the chair, fished out his keys and waited by the door.

"What's the plan?" she asked after shouldering her backpack.

"You'll take Code Blue and I'll follow you from a distance in my truck. That way, I can keep watch for anything unusual."

"I was about to suggest the same thing," she said. It was good they were on the same page. But then, there was a time when he would've sworn they could read each other's thoughts.

The minute she walked over to him, he opened the door and held it.

"Thank you," she said as she ambled by. "Give me a minute head start."

"I don't know where you work." He had to stand too close to her for longer than he cared to while she entered the address on his phone.

She shot him a look before saying, "Will I see you at the bar?"

"Not if I'm doing my job well." Garrett might not work in law enforcement like his brothers but he was one of the best trackers in the county. Hell, probably all of Texas if he listened to other people's opinions of him. But in all fairness, he needed to keep a distance from Brianna in order to stay focused. Because when she stood this close to him and he was breathing in her scent, he could easily get lost.

Garrett didn't do lost. He didn't do the kind of attraction that made him want to be a better person. And he didn't do the whole happily-ever-after lie.

Take his parents, for instance. Through no fault of their own they were dealt a hand that would cause most to shatter. His mother had been affected…no, was *still* being affected to this day by the child who was stolen from her. Would they go back and change their decisions if they'd known what was to come?

Being outdoors, Garrett could keep a clear head. He didn't want for anything. He didn't miss anyone. And he sure as hell didn't stay awake at night like his mother had on Caroline's birthday crying her eyes out.

Garrett stopped himself right there. The revelation came as a shock. He set it aside, figuring he could deal with it later. Brianna needed all his focus now and a minute had passed since she'd headed to her vehicle.

He started for his truck. His pulse kicked up a couple of notches with her being out of sight. He tried to convince himself it was because of the stalker but there was more to it than that. It fell into the category of "more stuff that needed to be kicked aside" for now.

Code Blue exited the parking lot as he cleared the apartment building. Brianna lived on the first floor.

He made a mental note to talk to her about that for her next move. She needed to live at minimum on the second floor for safety's sake. Burglars and rapists rarely risked a climb. For one, they could fall. For another, and this was probably the most important reason, they never risked getting seen scaling a building.

Garrett climbed into his truck. His gaze lingered on the empty passenger seat a second longer than he wanted it to. He started the engine and made the drive toward the bar. The ride was easy and there didn't appear to be any stalkers following her to work. Of course, this guy's pattern was to follow her home, which gave Garrett the impression the perp didn't know where she lived.

The blue hatchback could have followed her home from school. Why the bar?

The easy answer was the stalker was one of her customers, not one of her classmates. So, basically, he'd most likely been focused on the wrong thing. Except that didn't exactly feel right in his gut for some odd reason.

Most stalkers knew their victims. Would a customer at the bar know her?

Of course, they could be looking at a psycho she rejected. He should have asked her if she'd had to have anyone thrown out for harassment at the bar. But then, wouldn't she have mentioned that first?

Garrett pulled into a parking spot in the far end of the lot and waited. He would have to walk right past Code Blue to get to his ride later tonight. For now, there weren't many vehicles parked and he didn't want to be obvious that he was following her inside.

He had to take it on faith that once she got inside the building she'd be okay. He positioned his rearview mirror so that he could watch her as she exited her vehicle and walked toward the building. He also had to force his gaze from her sweet backside.

While he waited, he figured he could do a little more digging into the alpaca rescue to see what else he could find out. He fished out his cell phone and pulled up a search engine. He entered the name of the nonprofit. At least, he assumed it was a nonprofit.

Pulling up the website, he got a quick confirmation on the rescue's situation. Apparently, the owners had applied for nonprofit status. He made a note of their names, Randy and Susan Hanes. Made a quick joke about the underwear empire Randy must have come from.

Garrett cracked a smile at his own joke, bad as it was. Hey, stakeouts were boring. He'd had his fair share of them over the years while tracking poachers on family land, and others. The name was sticking in his craw. Hanes. Was it too obvious?

The thought it could be a fake sat heavy on the back of his mind. He could make a call or two and find out pretty quick but that would mean involving one or more of his brothers. Considering this case was at the forefront of everyone's mind, he'd be figured out in a heartbeat. Would he be putting his brothers in the line of fire? If this lead panned out, a killer could easily put his sights on the family again.

What about Garrett's mother? If anyone made a minor slip and let her in on it, could she handle it? She had to know all her children were investigating their father's murder. Granted, Colton and Cash were the obvious choices, but that was part of the reason Garrett saw it as his duty. His brothers had to follow protocol. They were almost too obvious. Garrett could handle the investigation his own way. No legal limits. No justice system handicapping him. He could get to the truth without the burden of filing paperwork or getting a judge's order.

He could also mete out his own sense of judgment. An eye for an eye?

Hold on right there. Garrett realized he was taking this too far. Maybe it was time to involve his brothers. Do everything by the book. Garrett wasn't worried about his life. It wasn't like he had anyone to come home to at night.

But death was too swift for the person who'd killed Finn O'Connor. And if Garrett killed someone wouldn't he end up the one in jail? He had to set his white-hot emotions aside on this one and think clearly. He couldn't run off half-cocked and act on impulse no matter how much he wanted to.

Garrett fisted his hands. He fisted and opened his fingers several times to try to ease the tension. His usual outlet of a hard day's work on a ranch wasn't available at the moment. He needed to find another way to blow off steam. And fast. Hopping out of his truck and firing off a few pushups would draw attention he couldn't afford.

A distraction would be nice about now.

Or he could call Colton. His brother might not even answer, especially the way Garrett had been treating the family.

With a deep breath, he pulled up his brother's contact from his list. Before he could talk himself out of it, he touched the screen and the call was in progress.

Colton picked up on the first ring.

"Everything okay?" The alarm in Colton's voice was a stark reminder of how little Garrett called.

"Yes, sure. I'm good," he said as casually as he could. "I had a question and I thought you might be a good resource. It's work related."

There was a beat of silence on the line.

"Okay." Colton drew out the word. "You know I'll do anything in my power to help, but I have to warn you that I'm bound—"

"I won't ask you to violate your oath." Garrett probably sounded a little defensive. His stress levels were rising based on how much more he was white knuckling the steering wheel.

"Then, what can I do for you officially?" Colton asked.

"A little research. I'm checking into a nonprofit for a friend and…" Garrett stopped himself right there. He wanted to tell Colton the truth. "I'm following up on a lead and I came across what I think is a bogus situation. I'd like to vet it out and don't have the first clue how to go about it."

"Is this in my jurisdiction, by chance?" Colton asked.

"Afraid not."

"Then, I have fewer resources and might have to call in a favor. But ask away. I'll do everything in my power to help." The resolve in Colton's voice inspired confidence in Garrett to move forward.

"I'm checking into an alpaca rescue and I think the name on the organization is bogus. The rescue is registered in the names of Randy and Susan Hanes," he said.

"As in the underwear company?" Colton's voice was laced with suspicion.

"My thoughts exactly," Garrett confirmed.

Colton chuckled. "Hanes isn't an uncommon name, though. Could be legit, but I'll check it out. I've come across some strange things in my years as sheriff."

"I bet you have." Garrett could only imagine what his brother had seen and probably done. He met his wife while on an investigation. He literally crashed into her car while in his service vehicle while she was on the run from a tainted cop.

"What's the name of the rescue and where is it located?" Colton asked.

Garrett provided the information along with a warning. "I have to tell you this might not be what it seems, and it could be dangerous to dig further into the details."

"That was a given when you reached out to me." The fact Colton didn't seem shocked or surprised made Garrett realize how often his brother faced dangers every day in his line of work.

The fact he could lose his brother without making

amends struck like a lightning bolt on a clear blue sky. At least part of his anger was tied to the same thing happening with his father.

And Garrett had loved the man. He had no idea how to live up to the O'Connor name but that didn't mean he didn't respect it. And now his father had gone to his grave without knowing how much Garrett respected him. The real kicker was that Garrett knew his father loved him. Finn O'Connor left nothing unsaid. He would have found a reason to be proud of Garrett even in the times he didn't give his father one.

So, the thought of that happening with Colton was a gut punch.

"I should be able to do a little digging on this one and come up with some answers for you," Colton said, breaking the silence.

"Much appreciated." Garrett realized how lame that sounded when he wanted to say so much more to his brother. The right words didn't come so he let a few more beats of silence sit between them.

"Is that everything?" Colton finally asked and Garrett could hear the questions in his brother's voice. To his credit, he didn't ask them. He seemed content to let Garrett do the driving on this conversation.

"Yeah, uh, actually, no. I did have something else I wanted to say." More of that cursed silence filled the line. "Since words aren't exactly my favorite thing—"

"They don't have to be. Just spit it out." The fact that Colton seemed to be gearing up to take a punch filled Garrett with regret.

"All I wanted to say was thank you." It was lame

but true and covered so much more than just this conversation.

"You're welcome, little brother." Colton hadn't strung that last pair of words in a sentence in far too long.

"I mean it, Colton. You're a great guy and I haven't always been…"

"Don't worry about it, Garrett. Seriously, it's all water under the bridge." Colton was being too nice, letting Garrett off the hook too easily.

Instead of making him feel better, it fired him up. "Hey. I'm not done here."

A beat of silence sat in between them again.

"I'm listening." Colton's voice turned dead serious.

"You've been a great big brother and I've given you nothing but hell. And while I can't promise I won't do the same thing in the future, I can say that I'm sorry about all the times I was a jerk." Garrett hadn't expected those words to roll off his tongue or to feel so freeing. It was suddenly like a chunk of the boulder that had been docked on his chest was lifting, releasing some of the pressure along with it.

"I won't argue the last part. There have been times when you've been a real pain in the backside," Colton said. "However, I will add that I wasn't always Mr. Wonderful on my end either. I goaded you into arguments when I knew better. So, if we're fessing up to the past, I have to take my fair share of the blame."

Garrett chewed on his brother's words for a minute. True enough, there were times when Colton was in the wrong. Why was it so easy to blame himself for every fight?

"Are we good?" Garrett asked.

"Always were on my end," Colton said like he meant it.

"Good. Because I don't want to go to my grave with words left unsaid."

"Whoa there. You need to back that statement up and explain. Does this have something to do with the research project I've taken on?" Colton asked.

"I've just been in my head a whole lot since Dad died. There was a whole lot I could have…" Garrett had to stop himself right there as he got choked up.

"I know what you mean." Colton's voice was low and filled with regret. Regret was something Garrett knew a little too much about. He'd recognize it from a mile away.

"Don't beat yourself up," Garrett said quickly. The irony wasn't lost on him. "I'm pretty good at doing that myself."

"Does it help?" Colton's question caught Garrett off guard.

"Not really. It usually leads to a spiral," Garrett admitted. Full disclosure was starting to release more of that tension balled up inside him.

"Sounds like hell." Colton's honest reaction caused Garrett to chuckle.

"It is." There was no use sugarcoating it.

"Then, why do we do it?" Colton asked.

"Maybe we have more in common than I realized,"

Garrett said. "I never would have guessed there was a real human underneath that Superman cape of yours."

The statement was only half true. It was meant to be a joke.

"That what you think?" Colton's defensive tone said it fell flat. "I'm some kind of superhero? Because I can promise you the opposite is t—"

"I wasn't saying it to offend you, Colton. But in my book, you always have been."

Colton let a couple of seconds go by before responding.

"When you put it like that, it sounds like a compliment," he said. "One I'd be proud to take."

Garrett ended the call with the promise to do a better job of keeping in touch. Out of the corner of his eye, he spotted a blue hatchback creeping down the side street.

Chapter Fifteen

The bar was prepped and Brianna had spent the past fifteen minutes in the bathroom freshening up before her shift.

Wanda came out of the second stall as Brianna pressed her lips together to even out her lipstick. The popular waitress sidled up to the sink next to Brianna's. The two weren't exactly buds but they worked well together. Meaning, Brianna didn't get in Wanda's way and vice versa. They shared a mutual respect for each other's jobs.

"What are you doing in here?" Wanda's face puckered up with the question.

"What? I'm not allowed to use the bathroom all of a sudden?" Brianna shot the woman her best offended look, even though she wasn't irritated at all. It was fun to tease Wanda.

"No. It's not that. It's just I never seen you in here before a shift, primping." Wanda pulled a tube of lip liner from inside her bra. Nice. She'd have to remember that move.

"Ah, this." Brianna zipped up her mini makeup

bag. She'd never kept one in her backpack before to-night, but there was no way she was admitting that to Wanda. Brianna would never hear the end of it. "Figured it would help with tips."

"Ah." Wanda nodded approval. "Here I was think-ing you had a man stopping by tonight."

"Me?" Brianna did her level best to pull off that same disgusted look but feared her flushed cheeks gave her away. She wanted to say, *not just any man,* but decided against it. She wasn't ready to share Gar-rett with anyone. Plus, she had no real designs on him anyway no matter how much her heart protested the thought, traitor that it was. Garrett was a friend who was helping her out. Period.

A quick glance at the mirror revealed that Wanda was studying her. Her cocked eyebrow said she wasn't buying the line. Another fib. Sort of. They were rack-ing up. The little dishonesties would take seed if she wasn't careful. The single piece of advice she'd been given by one of her customers, which had changed the way she thought, was to stand guard at her mind and be as careful of what she let inside as she let out. The tiniest weed could overtake the most beautiful garden.

She couldn't remember the man's name, or it was possible he never told her, but she could pick him out of a lineup to this day if she had to. Because she'd been wallowing in self-pity until that day. She didn't have it all figured out now, but she'd found a direc-tion in life and had gone all in. Before that, she'd been wandering, thinking she wasn't smart enough to go back to school or that she was too much older than her classmates. She had a powerful advantage that she'd noticed was lacking in many of the eighteen-year-olds she'd sat beside, and that was motivation.

"Probably not," Wanda finally said before adding a layer of ruby-red lipstick. She tucked the tube back inside her bra before shaking the "girls" a few times to let it settle.

"You're seriously going to have to show me how you do that one of these days," Brianna said, changing the subject.

"On last count, I have thirty-six more days," Wanda said wistfully.

Brianna was caught off guard that Wanda would care so much about her last day let alone keep a countdown.

"Yep. I'm almost out of here," Brianna said cheerfully. Too cheerfully. In fact, she was pretty certain it came off as insincere. She didn't want Wanda to feel bad.

"You're a solid bartender," Wanda said by way of compliment.

"Thanks. I like working with you too," Brianna said. She hadn't expected to get emotional about leaving this place. It was always a steppingstone to a better life. Then, she realized this *was* Wanda's life.

"Them classes you take. Are they expensive?"

"A little. Not as much as a four-year college," Brianna said. "I bet you could swing it if you picked up an extra shift here and there."

"You think?" Wanda gave herself a long, hard look in the mirror.

"I do. There's no question in my mind."

Wanda smiled before straightening her blouse to reveal a better look at her cleavage. "Maybe I'll check into it."

"You should." Then, Brianna added, "Or you could work in this castle for the rest of your life."

Wanda laughed. "You've just described hell."

"I guess I did." Brianna laughed too.

"See you out there on the floor," Wanda said walking out the door, but not before an eye roll.

"I'll be right out." Brianna wanted another second to pull herself together. Garrett's lead had been eating away at her all afternoon and evening. She didn't want to hold him up in any way from his father's investigation. Maybe she could convince him to take her along with him. She could get someone to cover her shift at the bar, figure out a way to make up the extra money. Or she could super hustle for tips tonight. She could admit to slowing down a little bit lately. Lack of sleep wasn't always great for the hustle.

She'd find a way to pitch the idea to him after work tonight.

After zipping up her makeup bag, she did a final mirror check before exiting the bathroom. Customers would be allowed inside in a few minutes. She had time to put away her makeup and perform one last check on supplies. Dan the man was her barback tonight. He was usually on point. Starting the night right usually determined how the next nine hours would go.

A great band was playing tonight. Texas Two-

Step would be on at nine o'clock and again at midnight. They were good about drawing a crowd. An uneasy feeling toyed with her stomach. The thought of a crowd didn't normally rattle her. Now that she'd picked up a stalker, it made her nervous. The creep could watch her from any corner and she'd be too busy to notice.

She could only hope the guy would move on to someone else. The thought of another woman going through this wasn't exactly reassuring, though. She thought about what Garrett had said about Professor Jenkins. Garrett was right. She couldn't allow the man to get away with trying to use his position to garner favors—and she knew exactly what he meant. A shudder rocked her body thinking about that man touching her; even incidental contact made her skin crawl.

No, she couldn't let him get away with it.

"Smiles on, ladies and gentlemen," Wade Horton said. "One minute till showtime."

Her manager really should work on Broadway. He had a flair for the dramatic and his skills seemed misdirected in a honky-tonk bar, even one as big and reputable as this one. Folks came from all over to boot scoot across the dance floor to a homegrown band. The place was grand with a center bar in a big circle. There were two corner bars on opposite sides of the place, a sawdust dance floor along with a small stage for the band. She'd worked her way up to having her own bar. The center bar was where everyone trained, and shared tips from the jars. Here in the corner, she had her own slice of heaven and she didn't have to share it with anyone.

Brianna wouldn't have it any other way.

Shot ladies walked around, but Brianna had her regulars. Then, there were tourists but they only came this way if the line was too long at the main bar. Everyone who worked here knew the real money was in the corner bars. That, and waitressing. A good waitress like Wanda could bring in a boatload of money on a live band night.

Wade circled the main bar. She waved her arms high in the air to get his attention, smiled when she was successful.

He jogged over.

"Honey, we're about to start the show. What can I help you with?" Wade was in his early forties but he had the energy of a twenty-year-old. Too bad he looked older than his years.

"I need to switch shifts tomorrow night. Personal reasons." She threw in the last couple of words to stem any questions. She wasn't about to tell her boss that she had to check up on an alpaca farm believed to actually be a kidnapping ring.

"Fine. But you need to find someone to trade with." He sounded angry but it was just his way. If he was, he'd get over it fast. She'd never seen him hold a grudge longer than a few minutes.

"Done." She pulled out her cell and fired off a text to Brent. He was always looking for extra shifts and working the corner bar was a bump up from where he normally worked in the center. The response came before Wade had a chance to walk away. "Brent will cover for me."

She held up her cell as proof.

Wade nodded before waving a hand in the air and then moving on.

"Have a good show tonight, Wade," she hollered at his back.

He gave another wave.

Brianna would miss this quirky place, she thought. And then she laughed. No, she wouldn't. She wouldn't miss the cramps in her calves that came with running nonstop for eight- and nine-hour shifts. She wouldn't miss dripping with sweat by the end of the night. And she wouldn't miss having her backside patted as she walked through a crowded room to get more ice or take a break from the bar.

The doors opened and folks started filing in. There were lone cowboys, wannabe cowboys and a fair amount of couples. The women usually came in later in the evening, closer to the band's first set.

Brianna's first customer approached and he was quickly followed by two of her regulars. They each took stools, spreading out enough to leave an empty stool in between them. It was odd to look at each one of them as a potential stalker.

"What can I get you?" she asked customer number one as she pulled two longnecks from the ice bucket, twisted off the caps, and then set each down in front of her regular guys with a smile and a wink.

A thought struck. Was she too friendly? Had she led someone on?

She stopped herself right there. Doing her job meant she was friendly with customers. She never dated anyone from work or led anyone on. There was no way she was going to find a way to blame herself for someone else's actions. Period.

"What do you have on tap?" the newbie asked.

She rattled off the list and then waited for his response as he mulled over his choices. She quickly scanned the room, searching for Garrett. Disappointment caused her shoulders to deflate a little bit when she didn't see him.

The man was good at being a ghost. But then, he'd had reason to be. He used to tell her about trips he went on with his dad and brothers when poachers were on the family's land. It sounded dangerous to her. But he was casual about it. He'd describe it like it was nothing.

"I'll take the first one you said." The newbie settled on an ale.

"All right." Brianna got to work and pretty soon was in a rhythm. The night went by in a blur and she didn't see Garrett one single time. But she did look at everyone differently this evening. So much so, that one of her regulars asked her if everything was okay.

She'd explained that finals were coming up and that she was stressed about all the work she needed to do by the end of the semester. Her true regulars could tell when she was preoccupied.

They were good about it, though. Four of them had asked if they could buy her a drink after work.

They'd also said they knew she didn't date from work. A friendly drink was all they were offering.

"You need me to walk you to Code Blue after closing tonight?" Hammer the bouncer asked. She'd seen him twice tonight.

"Nah, I'll be okay. I'm parked close," she said, then added, "Just don't tell Wade on me."

"Wouldn't dare." Hammer crossed his heart.

She hollered a "thank you" mostly to his back as he half jogged, half speed walked in the opposite direction. And then she skimmed the bar again, searching for any sign of Garrett.

A knot formed in her stomach thinking something might have happened to him. Garrett was impulsive. Had he followed a lead and ended up in some kind of trouble? The old Garrett wouldn't hesitate to take off if instinct told him to do so. She'd seen changes in him recently, especially when he talked about his family. Good changes. She could only hope he wouldn't revert back to his old ways for both of their sakes.

A cowboy walked out of the men's room. His hat was low and she didn't get a good look at his face but there was something familiar about him. Was he one of her regulars?

It didn't matter much. He was making a beeline for the door.

Out of the corner of her eye, she saw him try the handle and then knock on the glass. Hammer had to let the guy out. The only door in and out used by the public locked every night at two religiously. No one got in or out but through Hammer.

Hammer. She needed to pick his brain to see if anyone matching Derk's description, or Blaine's for that matter, had come into the bar recently. Why hadn't she thought of asking before?

COWBOYS AND COUPLES were leaving the bar in droves. Garrett wanted to slip inside to check on Brianna. Something told him to stay put. He could do more good here in the parking lot than inside, he reasoned. He surveyed the area, looking for single-occupant trucks or anything that seemed suspicious.

The lot was a sea of F-150s and Dodge Rams. So, yeah, noticing a lone driver in a truck was only a little bit easier than finding a needle in a haystack. He ruled out couples and figured the driver would linger or find a reason to hang around late.

Garrett's interest stirred when a cowboy exited the bar late. He had to be let out by the bouncer, a hefty guy who would give Garrett a run for his money in a fight. Not that Garrett doubted he was the one who would come out on top. But he would know this guy had been there. Very few people caused that reaction in Garrett, so he paid attention to it.

The cowboy kept his head down as he made a beeline to his… Volkswagen?

Garrett mentally crossed this cowboy off the list. Besides, what were the chances he'd go for a repeat this quickly? Slim to none. Garrett was getting antsy because he wanted Brianna out of danger and, if he was being honest, he wanted to follow up on the lead about the alpaca farm.

At least Colton was working behind the scenes to find out if Randy and Susan Hanes were legitimate people and the nonprofit was aboveboard. Those two things would inform him about what he faced. It was a start and he could build from there.

Plus, they had Derk's address now and Garrett wanted to make a stop. The blue hatchback from earlier was a dead ringer for the one in the school parking lot and Garrett wanted to ask the guy a few questions. Being in the school parking lot wasn't exactly against the law. Neither was driving past a bar. Unless this guy had another vehicle at his disposal and used it to torture Brianna.

Speaking of whom, Garrett had been on pins and needles all night. He'd been miserable. And Brianna had everything to do with it. The question was…what did he plan to do about it?

Nothing, he thought, ignoring the little voice in the back of his mind determined to call him a coward.

Chapter Sixteen

Brianna took two steps out of the bar and scanned the parking lot. Garrett couldn't decide if her expression was concern or fear from this distance. He didn't like either. She deserved to be happy. No, more than that, she deserved to have everything she wanted and more. He shouldn't be bothered by the fact she was settling for a nine-to-five life. He shouldn't care one iota.

So, why was he going to lose sleep over it tonight?

He climbed into the driver's seat of his truck, keeping one eye on Brianna when a knock on his passenger window startled him. He cut his gaze over faster than a barrel-racing horse.

None other than the bouncer stood there.

"Could I have a word with you, sir?" A very angry, very determined face stared at Garrett.

"Right now?" Garrett asked before thinking.

"Yes. Now." There was a finiteness to the bouncer's tone that said he'd stand in front of or in back of the truck if Garrett engaged the gearshift.

He had no choice but to step out of his vehicle and

meet the bouncer at the back in the dark lot where Garrett could try to keep an eye on Brianna. He could only hope that she would stay put until he settled this matter.

"My name's Garrett O'Connor and I'm a friend of Brianna's." Garrett stuck his hand out.

The bouncer just stared at it, crossing his arms over a massive chest instead. "What business do you have with her?"

The guy oozed protective instinct. His heart seemed in the right place but, man, his actions were misguided.

"Brianna and I go way back," Garrett started but his words were met with a hand.

"I bet you do." His tone said the opposite was true. "What are you doing here?"

"Meeting her after her shift." Garrett was honest enough. He also puffed out his chest a little bit to let the bouncer know he wasn't about to back down. If they needed to fight to figure out who was in charge here, so be it.

No, Garrett thought. That was his old way of thinking. How many times had he gotten into it with one of his brothers, or his boss or a coworker? Dozens. He couldn't think of one time where approaching a situation with anger actually made it better. Sure, there was the momentary rush of winning an argument or a fistfight, of being in the right and proving it. But it never worked out long term. All it ever did was alienate him from the people he cared about and/or the people he worked with.

He took in a deep breath, figuring it might not help but it surely couldn't hurt. Bouncer, on the other hand, fisted his hands at his sides.

Garrett decided to at least try to defuse the situation.

"I think we're getting off on the wrong foot here." Garrett couldn't exactly fault the man for just doing his job and looking out for Brianna. "Brianna and I grew up together and ran into each other last night at the gas station. She'd just left the police station and seemed out of sorts. We hadn't seen each other in years, so it was pretty random. But we were close once and she was shaken up."

Bouncer's eyebrow shot up. His hands relaxed at his sides. "She didn't say anything about being followed home last night."

"No? We can call her over and ask her, if you want. Or, better yet, I can give her a call." He made a move to fish his cell phone out of his front pocket, but Bouncer reacted quickly, moving his hand behind his back where Garrett was certain the man had a gun.

"Whoa there. I'm just reaching for my cell phone so we can give Brianna a call." Garrett held his hands in the peace position, palms up.

Bouncer nodded and said, "Move slow."

"No problem, man." Garrett was careful not to make any sudden movements despite his frustration that Bouncer was drawing attention to them. If someone was watching, he'd be busted. Using two fingers, Garrett eased his phone from his pocket. "See. Just my cell."

Bouncer nodded.

"I didn't catch your name, man," Garrett said as he pulled up her contact.

"My name's Jeff but everyone calls me Hammer on account of my last name being Hamm."

"What do you like to be called?" Garrett asked. Having a nickname and choosing a nickname were often two different things.

"Jeff."

"Okay, cool. Jeff, I can call Brianna right now and settle this or you can take my word and call her yourself. She's pulling out of the parking lot and it's my job to see that she gets home safely. It's your call." Garrett had never tried reasoning with anyone before. He could only hope it worked.

Jeff studied Garrett for a long moment. He glanced over at the empty spot that used to be occupied by Code Blue.

"Go on. And, man, keep our girl safe."

Garrett nodded but he didn't like the thought of sharing Brianna with anyone, not even a decent guy like Jeff. Because if given the chance, Jeff would take a promotion from protector/friend to boyfriend in a heartbeat if the offer was on the table.

Speaking of heartbeats, Garrett's pounded the inside of his rib cage. He rounded the truck in record time and reclaimed the driver's seat. He turned the key in the ignition and got nothing. For a split second he thought Jeff had come over to distract Garrett.

But the guy seemed genuine and that couldn't be faked. Garrett had dealt with more than his fair share of criminals in the poaching world and had worked beside a few on various ranches. He generally knew a bad actor when he saw one. It was always in the eyes.

Garrett bit out a string of curse words as he tried one more time to start the truck. Got nothing but click, click, click. Strange because he'd replaced the battery last month. He darted out of his vehicle after pressing the button that unlocked the hood lever.

"What's going on?" Jeff asked, rounding the front of the vehicle.

"I'm guessing someone unplugged my battery cables while we were talking." Wouldn't have been the easiest ploy, but a smart man could have timed the opening and closing of the hood with the crunch on gravel as cars left the lot, and the lighting out here kept everything in the shadows. It wasn't a tough fix but also gave the jerk an advantage. Garrett palmed the cell he'd tucked in his pocket a few minutes ago. He pulled up Brianna's name from his contacts and touched the screen.

The next two rings were the longest of his life. He fixed his cables while he waited, and slammed the hood shut. She finally picked up before the call rolled into voice mail.

"Hey, you sure are doing a good job of hiding because I haven't seen you all night," she immediately said.

"You are about to have company," he said. "Someone tampered with my vehicle."

Garrett gave a nod toward Jeff, who clenched his jaw so tight it looked like he might crack his back teeth. He'd been used and now someone he cared a lot about was in danger.

"Oh, no. Are you okay?" The fact she was trying to mask the fear in her voice was a gut punch.

"I'm on my way. Did you stick to the route?" he asked.

"Yes." She paused. "I see headlights coming up fast on my bumper."

By the time Garrett heard the *clunk*, he was spewing gravel underneath his tires trying to get out of the parking lot like his truck had wings. Jeff was already jogging toward the bar, or maybe it was his vehicle. He and Garrett hadn't exactly planned their next steps once they realized what had happened.

Someone knew enough about trucks to open Garrett's without drawing attention. He had to be somewhat handy with vehicles.

"I'm going to hang up and call 911 for you," Garrett said calmly. Based on the sound of her voice, she was in shock.

"Okay." She gasped a moment before the second *clunk*.

There was no way she could have gotten very far. They'd mapped out her route beforehand, so he figured she wasn't ahead of him by much.

Then, he heard, as if she were speaking in the distance, "I can't find my phone, Garrett. It got knocked out of my hand when he hit me the second time."

The knot in Garrett's stomach twisted tighter and he struggled to breathe for a second or two. He had to call the cops but he hated getting off the phone with her. Cutting off his lifeline to Brianna was going to be hell.

Then, he realized he could call her back. She could answer through her vehi—never mind. Code Blue was too old-school for Bluetooth. Dammit.

"Call out the street names on the next intersection," he shouted.

No response.

"Garrett. Where are you?" she said before he heard tires squealing.

"I'm hanging up now. If you find your cell, call me back." He had no choice but to end the call with her no matter how much it tightened the knot. He told himself he would call her back and the sound of her phone ringing might help her locate the cell.

He ended the call trying not to focus on the fact he was cutting off his lifeline to her. Then he dialed 911. The conversation with the dispatcher was short and sweet. He made a guess as to where Brianna might be and then got off the phone as quickly as he could after being told the nearest officer was a little more than fifteen minutes away. Jeff had held Garrett up five minutes and then the battery took another three or four. At this rate, Garrett would reach her long before the officer did. And that was only if she stayed on course, which was a fifty-fifty shot at this point. She might have had to veer off course to shake the guy who'd already hit her a couple of times.

Garrett instructed his phone to call Brianna. The phone rang once and his pulse kicked up a few notches. He would give just about anything, including his freedom, to hear her voice on the other end of that line. The second ring caused him to suck in a breath and hold it. The third sent his mind into a downward spiral because one more and his call would go straight to voice mail.

The sound of her voice on the line gave him a split second of hope until he realized he'd just transferred into voice mail.

Garrett issued a sharp sigh. This wasn't a good sign. He white knuckled the steering wheel as he blew through a stop sign. Brianna never took the highway even though it would be faster. She never trusted Code Blue to make it.

The feeling he'd let her down in the worst possible way engulfed him. He couldn't afford to let it take hold. Renewing their friendship, or whatever label worked, was the best thing that had happened to him in far too long.

Garrett gripped the steering wheel a little tighter and made the call again. This time, it went to voice mail on the first ring.

BRIANNA BIT BACK a curse as she wheeled left, practically rolling up on two tires as she made a hard left. She needed to get Code Blue back onto the agreed-upon path home. Garrett would have called the law by now and he would tell them where she was supposed to be.

The truck roaring up to her bumper again was relentless and all this swishing around might empty what little gas was left in her tank. There was a hole the size of a baseball she'd been meaning to have fixed. Car repairs fell behind classes, books, rent and food.

Anger roared through her and she had half a mind to stop her vehicle right there in the middle of the road just to see what this jerk planned to do next. In fact, that's what she did. She knew she couldn't keep going with him bumping her every few minutes. It was inevitable he'd stop her somehow. She'd rather be in control of that action.

She jammed her foot on the brake and prepared for impact. The screech of rubber tires against pavement caused her to tense up. She'd been told by one of her customers that if she was ever in an accident she should relax. How on earth did anyone relax when they were about to be slammed?

The impact never came. She risked a glance in the rearview mirror as the truck slowed down just as quickly.

"Come on, you sonofabitch. Make your move," she bit out. She probably shouldn't play this game but, man, she was so tired of running from this guy. Law enforcement was no help.

Brianna took that back as she fingered the charm hanging from her necklace. She could hear sirens wailing in the night air. They couldn't be too far away, which meant she hadn't gotten too far off track while trying to shake this creep. She took the opportunity to punch the gas pedal as she recited a quick protection prayer she remembered from the few times she'd been taken to church in grade school.

The charm had finally worked. Or maybe Garrett was good luck to have around. Either way, she planned to take advantage of the opportunity to leave this jerk in the dust.

"Eat my gravel," she said as she mashed the pedal as hard as she could.

Code Blue did its best impression of a race car, which wasn't much. But she made it around the corner and toward the wailing siren without the truck catching up to her. The truck behind her made the first turn in the opposite direction.

"I thought so," she said under her breath, not ready to risk him changing his mind. She moved toward the glorious sound of help, wishing she'd gotten a look at the guy. There weren't a whole lot of streetlights in the small towns surrounding the bar and this was no exception. At least she had a direction and a diversion.

The adrenaline rush started to fade and her hands shook on the wheel. It didn't take long to find the officer. She flashed her lights and then cut them off. She stood up, waving her arms in the air.

A truck roared up from behind and her heart dropped into her toes as panic gripped her. And then she realized who was behind the wheel. Garrett. She couldn't get out of Code Blue fast enough as an SUV, lights twirling, barreled toward her.

The look on Garrett's face would stick in her mind for a long time. Worry lines etched his forehead and bracketed his mouth. The sheer panic in his eyes as he raced toward her nearly cracked her chest in two.

A second or two later, she was burying her face in his chest, thinking this was the best spot in the world for her right now.

Chapter Seventeen

Garrett held Brianna as she gave her statement to the officer, giving a description of the truck and pointing to where it took off as he relayed the information. Her body trembled even though it wasn't cold outside and he'd wrapped a blanket around her shoulders. It was most likely from adrenaline, so she wasn't in any real trouble physically. He didn't plan to let her out of his sight moving forward, though.

How stupid had he been? He never should have allowed her to drive home on her own, never should have let her take that risk. He'd been naive to think he could handle this on his own without involving law enforcement or grabbing one of his brothers.

There were situations that required him not running off half-cocked and playing lone wolf. His mistake could have cost Brianna her life. He never would have forgiven himself if anything had happened to her.

When she was finished giving her statement, he gave his. It was short and to the point. He asked for a recommendation for a reputable towing company in the area before the officer retreated to his vehicle. Garrett moved Brianna inside his truck before grabbing her things from Code Blue. He felt around on the floorboard for her cell phone and found it. Then, he used his own to pull up the towing company name before making a quick call to have Code Blue picked up. No way was he risking getting caught behind another vehicle or a red light that would cause them to end up separated. Not again.

He climbed into the driver's seat and then got back on the road to her place, stewing on his mistakes.

"Thank you for thinking so quickly and calling the law." Brianna broke the silence.

"I almost got you killed," he quickly countered. "You shouldn't be thanking me."

She was silent for a beat. Then came, "I know you, Garrett. You can be one intense person. But there's no way you would intentionally put me in harm's way. I doubt you'd let a fly land on me, let alone allow some raving lunatic to cause me any pain."

"And yet look what happened," he ground out. "I failed. You were alone and scared."

"None of which was your fault," she said calmly. There was no reason to rise to his frustration level. He was really only upset with himself and she hated that he blamed himself.

"Not true," he said in a low growl.

"Garrett, I want you to listen here. Okay?" She touched him on the shoulder. "Really listen."

He grunted a yes.

"I probably would be hurt or worse right now if it

wasn't for you. Whoever that creep is, one thing is clear. He set his sights on me for one reason or another. We may never know why. It could be my wheat-colored hair—" she flipped a tuft in the air "—so I won't let you take responsibility for some jerk-off's actions. You hear me?"

As much as he appreciated her honesty, he couldn't get past his own failure.

"You are one of the best people I've ever met and I won't let you beat yourself up over this," she contended. Granted, she made a good argument. A logical one. He was burning on pure emotion right now.

He wasn't quite ready to let himself off the hook no matter how much sense she made.

"How many people do you know who would set their own life aside based on running into an old friend at a gas station when she looked like she needed a hand up?" There was a lot more ire in her voice now.

"Probably a few," he countered, but he knew how weak his own argument was.

"Nope. Not even a few. Not even two. In fact, I'd bet the farm that there weren't a whole mess of people *besides* you who would do that for someone who was basically a stranger." Her temper was climbing and he needed to calm her down.

The best way to do that was to make a joke. So, that's exactly what he did, praying it wouldn't fall flat.

"You underestimate how freakin' hot you are," he quipped, hoping she would take the bait.

Brianna burst out laughing. And then so did he.

She reached over and gave him a playful jab in the arm. "I'm going to remember you said that, Garrett O'Connor. You can't take that one back."

Good. Because he had no intention of trying.

When the laughter died down, she said, "I took off work tomorrow so we could visit the alpaca farm together."

"Absolutely not." He was shaking his head no before she even finished her sentence.

"Hear me out before you decide," she hedged.

He took in a sharp breath. Her voice had the tone it always had when she'd made up her mind and was about to win an argument. It was good to know more than a few things hadn't changed about her.

"I'll listen, but that's as far as I'm promising," he said.

"Well good. That's all I asked." She continued before he made a smart-aleck remark they both knew was coming. "If you go there alone, it'll look suspect. Think about it. How many grown men do you see at an alpaca farm on a Friday morning?"

"Probably not many."

"And you don't want to draw attention to yourself. Am I right?" She practically beamed because she knew she had him.

"No, I don't."

"Then, we'll go as a couple. Women fall for that sappy stuff all the time. We can pretend we're on a date and they'll never be the wiser." She sat a little bit straighter, clearly pleased with her argument.

And since he couldn't shoot any holes in it, he agreed.

"One condition," he said.

"Not if it's to tell me I have to stay in the car," she argued.

"Did I say that?" he asked.

"No." She practically sulked and it was about the damned sexiest pout he'd ever put his eyes on.

"But we'll both have to stay in the car," he needled her.

"What?" It seemed to dawn on her when she brought her hands down to slap the seat. "Are you kidding me right now?"

"Would I do that to you?" He wanted to keep the mood light and reduce her stress levels. She'd been in full panic mode before despite keeping her cool.

"It's a drive-through animal encounter, isn't it?" She made air quotes with her fingers when she said the word *encounter*.

"Yes, ma'am."

"So, we really are both staying in the car," she said.

"That about sums it up." He nodded, enjoying the fact he got her to a place where she could kid around again. Brianna deserved a life that made her laugh freely every day. Hands down, her laugh was music to his ears.

Before he got all poetic, he decided to add, "There's a gift shop, though. I'd be happy to buy you a stuffed alpaca."

"And we can snoop around." She wiggled her eyebrows.

"Only if I get the all clear from Colton."

"You told him?" There was straight-up shock in her voice.

"Figured it was time to let him in a little. You know?" He pulled into a visitor's spot near her building.

"Wow. What can I say, Garrett?" She paused for a second. "Would it sound trite if I said I was proud of you?"

"Not at all. In fact, it means a whole lot to hear you say those words." He couldn't help himself. He broke into a wide smile. "He's checking into the background of the so-called owners to see if they are legit. He doesn't know the whole story yet but I plan to fill him in while we're on the way there at first light. Are you certain you can miss class?"

"This once won't tank my grade." She reached over and squeezed his forearm. The move shouldn't send a lightning bolt straight to his heart and it sure as hell shouldn't be so sexy.

Fighting his instincts to pull her close and claim those full lips of hers again, he issued a sharp sigh before exiting the driver's side of the vehicle and jogging over to the passenger door. He opened it and helped her climb out.

"My legs are weak," she said.

"It's all the adrenaline wearing off. It does a real number on your body. Lean on me, Brianna. I won't let you fall."

She didn't look up at him right away, but when she did the tears welling in her eyes were a knife to his heart. From what he gathered so far, there weren't a whole lot of people she could depend on in her life. He'd become one. He wanted to be one.

Inside her apartment, she walked straight to the bedroom and he fought himself once again to keep from following her. The sounds of the spigot turning on didn't help. All that did was put naked images of her in his thoughts.

With some effort he normally didn't have to pull on, he pushed those images aside. It was too late to reach out to Colton now. Garrett would call his brother first thing in the morning. It wouldn't hurt to fill him in on both situations. See what his brothers could do to help.

This whole territory was foreign to Garrett, but he was beginning to see the error of his ways. Shame he had to lose a father before getting the gut punch he'd needed for a few years now. Not that his absence from the family was anyone else's fault. He owned his mistakes. The trick was not letting them own him.

Brianna didn't fall into the same category. She was the most "right" thing that had happened to him in a long while.

BRIANNA FINISHED OFF her shower by making the water as cold as she could stand it. Because one seriously hot man was in the next room and she needed to cool her jets. Plus, she'd watched a show on the nature channel once that said a brush with death kicked in a primal instinct to procreate. So, the fact she wanted to have sex with Garrett more than she wanted to

breathe could be chalked up to nature's desire to pre-
serve itself. Or something like that. Or maybe it was
replicate itself. Who knew?

Being of sound mind, she had enough sense not
to act on the desire. Because on a primal level she
knew sex with Garrett would change things for her
and she wasn't just talking about their relationship.
She knew on instinct it would set the bar so high for
all future sex no one could live up to it.

She dressed in her least revealing pajamas, literally her Christmas fleece, and then came out into the
living area holding a spare towel.

"Your turn." She handed the towel over ignoring
the hungry look in his eyes that made warmth circu-
late through her. She broke eye contact as fast as she
could to stay in neutral territory.

"Thank you." Garrett took the offering and she
tried her best not to imagine him naked in her shower.
He had the kind of sculpted body normally reserved
for athletes who were on top of their game. He came
by his through hard work and had the calloused hands
to prove it. He had those rough hands she could only
dream about against her skin. A thrill of awareness
skittered across her body at the thought.

Coffee. She needed caffeine. The long shift was
taking its toll and if she crashed now, it would be
lights out for half the day. Every muscle in her body
ached at this point. A few hours of sleep would only
anger her tired bones. She'd learned a long time ago
that staying awake after a long and busy shift was the
only way to make it to a morning class.

Plus, she wanted to be wide awake for the alpaca farm trip. The two of them had more catching up to do on the drive and she wanted to know what Garrett had been working on in all these years since she'd moved away from Katy Gulch. It might just be the extreme situation or the fact they'd been apart so many years but she could swear she was seeing changes in him. The old Garrett would never have called in his brother, especially not Colton.

Not having siblings of her own, she always thought it was a shame the two of them didn't get along better. All she'd had growing up were her parents. Life had hardened them both in different ways, so basically, she had herself to rely on. There was no extended family to help. Neither of her parents were close with their families. She didn't grow up with large gatherings for the holidays. Which made living in Katy Gulch special to her. There, she'd had friends who she counted as family. The community had been tight-knit. Moving away had been akin to cutting all ties with her world.

Between school and her rebellious years, she'd lost touch with everyone from the small town where she'd spent some of the best years of her childhood. How many times had she dreamed of getting a nine-to-five close enough to town to be able to buy a small place of her own there?

More than she could count. More than she cared to count. More than she knew better to count.

Garrett emerged from the bathroom at almost the exact moment the coffee finished brewing.

"You couldn't have better timing." She chuckled as she held up the fresh pot. Looking at him while he was wrapped in nothing but the towel she'd given him a few minutes ago was something she knew better than to do. "I'll fix a couple of to-go cups for us."

"Smells like heaven." He retrieved a small toiletries bag from the duffel he'd tucked to one side of the couch. "I'll be done in a sec."

He probably picked up a fresh outfit too but there was no way she was staring at him long enough to find out. He was pure temptation when she needed to keep a clear head. The few kisses they'd shared already occupied too much real estate in her thoughts. Her cheeks flushed just thinking about them.

Coffee. She poured two cups and then took a sip of hers, enjoying the burn on her throat.

Finals would be happening soon and she needed to come up with a plan to get through the next thirty-five days with her sanity intact. She thought about Code Blue. Her Jeep wasn't in great shape but that vehicle was Brianna's lifeline.

The clock read four-thirty in the morning. She needed to change already into something more appropriate for a drive-through animal encounter. Skipping class wasn't ideal but this had to take priority. The place was perfect cover for any kind of kidnapping ring when she really thought about it. It would be off the beaten path but registered. Then, there was the fact people would be coming and going all day. How easy would it be to drive a van full of kids there? Or take them out one by one. Potential adopters could literally drive up and take a child home. No one would question couples coming in or families going out.

The trick would be hiding from the government. But how many raids were there on alpaca farms? As long as the animals were well cared for there would be no reason to call in the Texas Department of Agriculture, or whatever agency was responsible.

As soon as Garrett exited the bedroom, she set her to-go mug on the counter and then hopped into action.

The sound of the door opening and closing got her legs moving into the living room from the bedroom where her door was closed. Garrett was gone. And so was his coffee mug.

Chapter Eighteen

Movement behind Garrett's truck caught his attention as he started out of the lot. He slammed on his brakes so he wouldn't hit whatever it was that had crept up behind him. A thunk sounded against his tailgate anyway, and he immediately figured out who was responsible.

He hopped out of the driver's seat and left the door open as he walked back to confront a red-faced Brianna, standing in back of his truck.

"What do you think you're doing, Garrett O'Connor? We had a deal and if I can't trust you then—"

He stopped her by claiming her mouth. She put her fists up against his chest but seemed to have forgotten why. The next second, she planted her flat palms against him and pushed. He took a step back to brace himself.

"That's not playing fair and you know it." Her stubborn streak was a mile long.

"Believe it or not, I wasn't planning to take off. I noticed an air station at the front of your apartment and figured I'd check the tires before we hit the road." He quirked a smile.

Her mouth formed an O.

"I wouldn't do that to you, Brianna." He was trying to keep the mood light but he'd seen the look of betrayal in her eyes. It was one she seemed a little too acquainted with. Again, he thought about the situation with her mother's affair, pondering how odd it was how much these traumas stuck in life. No matter how much time passed, the hurt could so easily resurface. "Can you learn to trust me?"

She stood there for a long moment before answering, looking hard into his eyes.

"I'll give it my best shot, Garrett. It's not always easy for me." She issued a sigh. "But I do realize how unfair it is to put all my past pain on you." She grabbed a fistful of his shirt and tugged at it. "I know how you used to be and I figured not much has changed."

He must've worn his hurt on his sleeve because she quickly put her hands up in the surrender position, palms toward him.

"But that's not true. You have changed. You're making amends with your family. You've been nothing but kind to me. And you've held your temper when it would have exploded in the past," she said.

Those words were balm to a damaged heart. Being with her made him want to be a better person—the person reflected in her eyes when she really looked at him.

"So, yes, I'll trust you," she continued. "And I

promise not to keep waiting for you to hurt me or desert me."

"Then, I vow to live up to your expectations. This friendship means the world to me, Brianna." There was a flash of emotion across her gaze when he spoke those words—an emotion he couldn't quite put his finger on for how quickly she recovered.

"Friends it is." She stuck her hand out between them.

"We can do better than that." He took it and used it as leverage to haul her against his chest. He brought his free hand up and then ran his finger along her jawline.

"I'll grab my coffee and lock up." She sucked in a breath before ducking out of his grasp. "Will you wait for me right here?"

"You got it," he said. She'd done the right thing. They kept blurring the line between friendship and... what? Casual sex? Friends with benefits?

He had no doubt having sex with Brianna would be mind-blowing. And yet, he also knew on instinct once wouldn't be nearly enough. Not with her.

Garrett sat on that thought while he reclaimed the driver's seat and waited. A few minutes later, she bounded down the stairs and his chest clenched at the sight of her in a casual outfit of jeans and a cream-colored lacey tank top underneath a cropped sweater. She got to the passenger side before he could exit the vehicle to open her door for her but she didn't seem to mind. She climbed into the cab and then positioned her travel mug in the cup holder. Her fresh-flower-and-citrus scent filled the space, filled his lungs.

What could he say? The woman took his breath away.

"What?" She seemed genuinely confused as to the effect she could have on a person.

Since they were trying to keep their relationship in the friendship zone, he smiled and shook his head as he put the gearshift in Reverse.

It didn't take long to check the tires, fill up the tank and get on the highway.

"I was frazzled last night and didn't think to ask where the tow truck was taking Code Blue," she said as he found a steady speed. Texas highways were notorious for their fast speed limits and this one was no exception.

"I had her towed to the nearest reputable body shop. I hope you don't mind," he said.

"Not at all. An estimate never hurt anyone, right?" she quipped.

"I didn't ask for one. Told them to go ahead and fix her up for you." He knew he was walking a tightrope with this one. Brianna wasn't the kind to take advantage of others and she might see this as charity. She would hate to be considered a charity case.

The silence in the cab ratcheted up his pulse a couple of notches.

"Okay." She drew out the last letter. "I guess I can find a way to stretch my bank account. A little heads-up would have been nice."

"Any chance you'd allow me to cover the charges?"

he asked, then quickly added, "Not as some kind of charity but for a graduation gift."

She took her time answering and the suspense was killing him.

"I don't see any harm in accepting a gift for graduation." She raised her eyebrows. "But you do know that I haven't actually graduated yet."

"You will, though. Consider this an early present," he added.

"It's really nice of you, Garrett. And very generous. Let me know how much it is and I can go in halves on it once I get on my feet after my new job," she said.

"Or we could work something else out," he offered.

She tweaked his arm. "Garrett O'Connor—"

"Before you get too upset, I'm only suggesting you can help with my family's website. Do a little pro bono work. What do you think?" he asked.

"That would be all right," she agreed. She pulled out her phone.

He had an ulterior motive with the exchange. It meant he would need to be in contact with her and possibly get to see her again once this was all over.

"It's a good website, though. I'm not real sure you need my help," she stated.

"It's the same website we've had for the past decade. It needs a facelift," he continued. He was determined to pay for the cost of Code Blue's repairs one way or another. This was the easiest way to get her to agree to let him.

"Okay. I'll take a deeper look on my laptop later. The bones of the site are good, though."

Pride filled his chest at the compliment.

"Have you thought about where you'll look for a job once you get out of school?" he asked.

"Anywhere they'll take me." She laughed. "This is probably going to sound stupid to you considering you've spent the last decade trying to get away from Katy Gulch, but I'm hoping to get a job nearby. I'd love to have a small place on the outskirts of town."

"Doesn't sound out of the realm of possibility at all." It was selfish to want her to live close to his home—a home he appreciated more and more with every passing day.

His cell buzzed, cutting into their conversation.

"It's Colton." He hit the button on the steering wheel that answered the call.

"Wow," she said low and under her breath, sounding impressed with the technology in his truck. He'd buy her a brand-new Jeep if she'd let him, but there was no way he'd win that battle. Fixing up Code Blue would have to do for now. Besides, her vehicle had a whole lot of sass and charm, and he sensed she had an emotional attachment to it.

He understood. He still owned his first truck. It was at the ranch, parked at the home his mother had built for him when he was of age.

Recently, his mother had allowed Caroline's place to be used by the occasional guest and it had fired him up, made him think she'd given up on finding her daughter.

"Hey, Colton," Garrett said. "I'm here with Brianna Adair."

"Hi to you both," Colton said before adding, "Brianna, it's been too long."

There wasn't a hint of wistfulness or regret in his brother's voice about Brianna. Water under the bridge? Or was it the fact Colton had a beautiful new wife and a pair of twins most in the family thought hung the moon? Probably all of the above. His brother had found true love with Makena, and Garrett was nothing but happy for them both. Locking down with the right person had made Colton the happiest Garrett had ever seen his brother. Makena had stepped into the role of mother to the twins like they were her own children, which was much needed considering their birth mother had been killed in a tragic car accident not long after their births.

"Thanks, Colton," she said. "It's good to hear your voice again."

"Same," Colton said without a hint of jealousy in his voice. There shouldn't be, but Garrett couldn't deny it made him happy to confirm.

"What's up?" Garrett asked.

"I'm glad you're awake," Colton started. "You were right to question the names on the nonprofit. It turns out Randy and Susan Hanes were an actual couple. They passed away fifteen years ago in the same nursing home within days of each other. Whoever is using their names is pulling off a scam."

"I knew something felt off." Garrett had learned a long time ago to trust his instincts. They were usually backed by experience and he'd come across plenty of folks running from their past in various bunkhouses during his ranching career.

"Which leads me to my next question." Colton hesitated. "Does any of this have to do with Dad?"

"It might. We're heading that way now to check out the place. See if anything else fishy pops up." Garrett could have lied to Colton. What good would it do? His brother wasn't stupid and he had to realize what Garrett was going after. They all were working on the case in some way or another.

"Okay. Keep me posted if you find anything," was all Colton said.

Shock momentarily robbed Garrett's voice.

"Will do, big brother." Garrett coughed to clear his throat.

"Be careful out there. Kidnapping rings are nothing to play around with. I know I don't have to tell you that and you have certainly dealt with vicious criminals before, but…" Colton seemed to get a little choked up. Garrett chalked it up to the emotions that were still raw after losing their father. "We don't know what we're dealing with here yet."

"You know I will." He glanced over at Brianna. "I have a lot to live for and there's no way I'd put Brianna in harm's way. This is solely a fact-finding mission. I plan to get in and then get out."

"If this pans out, it'll be the closest any of us have come to finding out who killed Dad," Colton stated. "I hope it does."

"Me too."

"Do you need anyone to head that way for backup?" Colton asked.

"Not right now. Like I said, I have no plans to poke the bear if I find trouble here. We'll get in and get out, and then leave the rest to qualified law enforcement personnel. I didn't say anything before because there isn't much to say right now," Garrett explained.

"If you need any one of us, I'll have a chopper on standby," Colton said. "What's the point of all this family money if we don't use it to take care of our own?"

"I'll give you a call as soon as we leave the property," Garrett promised. It was odd to realize someone else had his back. Odd in a good way. Garrett realized just how stubborn he'd been all these years to think he had to go at life alone. But then, maybe he did. How else would he know what he'd been missing?

They ended the call after saying goodbyes. More of those layers of armor encasing Garrett's heart cracked when he thought about how much of a jerk he'd been. All he could say was, experience was the best teacher and he'd had plenty being a lone wolf. What could he say? It was time to play another song.

THE ALPACA FARM would be easy to miss if someone didn't absolutely know where they were going, Brianna thought as Garrett drove down a long, twisty road. A dust cloud kicked up by the tires was so dense that a car could be ten feet behind them and they'd never know.

Sure made it easy for someone to see them coming too.

"We should seem like a couple," Brianna said, taking off her seat belt to scoot into the middle. Being close to Garrett was always risky, especially when his spicy scent filled her senses. Self-control was her middle name. Brianna held back a grin. It usually was. When it came to being with Garrett, it was more like a goal.

He took his right hand off the wheel and looped his arm around her shoulders. She leaned into it as he pulled up to the front gate.

There was a hut in front of what looked like a ten-to-twelve-foot fence with another foot of barbed wire at the top.

A guy who looked more like a security guard than a ticket seller stepped out of the hut. He had on all khaki-colored clothes and she noticed a holster on his belt.

Garrett rolled down the window, bringing in a dust storm along with it. "Two tickets."

"That'll be sixty-five dollars," the guy said. His face was sun worn and his eyes were shielded by reflective sunglasses.

Garrett reached into his pocket and pulled out a stack of folded-up twenties. He peeled off three and then located a five-dollar bill.

"All right. Follow the signs and don't leave your vehicle or the trail. Keep your speed down below ten miles per hour at all times." He pointed to a camera. "We have several of those around the park. Just because you can't see us doesn't mean we can't see you. If you violate any of the rules, you will be escorted off the premises. Understood?"

This was straight up the strangest welcome Brianna had ever received.

"Got it," Garrett said casually. "Oh, and is there a gift shop for my girlfriend for after the trail?"

"Yep. Straight through that way. They sell food in case she wants to feed the animals. We have a strict policy on no outside food." He pointed to another sign with a big X on it across what looked like popcorn and peanut bags.

"Thanks a bunch," Garrett said before driving onto the property as the automatic gate opened. He rolled up his window as the gate immediately closed behind them.

"That guy was creepy," she said.

"I noticed that too. And what kind of park needs an armed guard at the gate?" It was more statement than question.

"I thought the same thing. He probably has a license." She figured that much would be on the up-and-up.

"It would be real difficult to surprise anyone in this operation," he noted. "But just in case they have listening devices planted around, we better hold off speaking any more about it until we're clear of here."

"Okay, good point." She chewed on her thumbnail as her pulse climbed.

He parked and put his hand over hers.

"We can take off if you're not comfortable here," he started.

"Sorry about the nervous habit." She put her hand in her lap. "I haven't done that in years. Guess this is catching me off guard."

"Are you okay with staying?" he asked.

"We didn't come all the way here for nothing, Garrett. I can pull it together."

He leaned in so close she thought he was going to kiss her. Instead, he said, "In case you're ever wondering, I think you're an amazing woman."

Didn't those words send her stomach free-falling?

"You're pretty amazing yourself," she said when she could catch her breath.

"Did you just call me pretty?" He was clearly teasing, and it did the trick.

She laughed.

"How do you do that?" she asked, unable to suppress her grin.

"Do what?" He was acting mighty innocent.

"Make me laugh so much. I swear I haven't laughed this much in years. And it's been a wild ride over the past twenty-plus hours. I don't even know how many anymore. I've lost count," she said.

"Being with someone who makes you laugh makes time fly by," he said. She wasn't sure if he was talking about him or her. Either way, it was a true statement. "We can go inside whenever you're ready."

She also realized he'd gotten this close to her to fill her field of vision. When she looked at him, and only him, her stress levels decreased dramatically.

"Let's go," she said.

He held up a finger before exiting his side of the vehicle and then jogging around to hers. They were supposed to be on a date and he sure was acting the part. The minute she stepped out of the truck, he hauled her against his chest and placed a tender kiss on her lips. Warmth spiraled through her, pooling between her thighs.

He was a little too good at getting her body to react to him. She needed to keep that in mind and close to her heart.

He linked their fingers and shot her a hundred-watt smile in a show of perfectly straight, perfectly white teeth. That smile could melt a glacier. It had already done a number on her heart.

Taking in a breath to bring in something besides his spicy scent, she nodded toward the building. "I hope they have a stuffed sloth in there. I've always wanted one of those."

"You do know this is an alpaca farm, right?" He squeezed her hand.

"That's all? I thought we were going to a ranch or something," she teased.

He pulled her in close, dropped her hand and then looped his arm around her waist. He held the door open for her and she led the way into the small shop filled with stuffed alpacas in various sizes, lava-lamp alpacas, postcards with alpacas and pretty much every color sweater with alpacas on them.

Garrett followed her around the shop, occasionally standing behind her with his hands on her shoulders. He leaned in for a sweet kiss here and there that smoldered with the promise of so much more if she let the wildfire rage.

It wasn't difficult to sell a relationship when their chemistry burned hotter than a campfire.

There was a young person working the shop. She looked to be around sixteen or seventeen and stood behind the cash register, reading a tattered novel.

"What looks good?" he finally asked.

"How about this one?" She picked up a baby alpaca.

"Looks good to me." He walked over to the cash register with her beside him. "How much for this one?"

The young girl looked at them with wide eyes. Fearful eyes?

Chapter Nineteen

"That one is twenty dollars plus tax." Wide brown eyes stared up at Garrett. This kid was barely old enough to drive and she had a resigned look on her face that would haunt him forever. Walking away from here without taking her with him was going to be one of the most difficult things he'd ever done.

He pulled out a twenty and a couple ones and set them down on the counter as she rang the item up. She glanced over her shoulder like she expected someone to come in from the back any moment. The way she kept checking gave him the impression she was scared.

She counted out his change and set it on the counter. "Can I get you a bag for that?"

"No, thanks," Brianna said, her voice a study in calm. He could almost read what she was thinking because he was mulling over the same thing. This kid didn't want to be here, and not in that bored, I-have-something-better-to-do-with-my-time teenager mode he'd seen too often. She didn't want to be here because she was scared. Forced?

He linked fingers with Brianna again and headed toward the exit, stopping in front of the door. He turned toward the register. "Do you have a map of the property by any chance?"

"It'll cost five dollars," she said, her voice frail.

He walked back over to her. While she turned to reach behind her, he checked her for bruises. The dress she wore was a size too big and she looked underweight for her frame. As she stretched her arm to reach the maps, he saw several purplish marks in various stages of healing. The long-sleeved dress was meant to cover them, just as he'd suspected.

Garrett ground his back teeth. This wasn't the time to act. He needed to think this thing through. Grab her now, and he would be helping her. But how many like her were in the back of this house? Or in a barn? It took everything inside him to walk out the shop door without that young girl. He paid her and thanked her for the map. He couldn't wait to get off the property and call Colton. At the very least, this kid was here against her will and being abused. Colton would know exactly what to do with the information.

Again, Garrett had to force a smile as he walked Brianna to the truck. This time, she squeezed his hand, letting him know she saw it too. He gave a subtle nod. Go about this the wrong way and he'd do more harm than good.

But the stringy-haired little girl would haunt his thoughts until he found a way to get her out of there.

The trail wasn't long, thankfully. Alpacas dotted the landscape. Garrett was ready to get off the property as fast as possible so he could get hold of his brother. Colton would be very interested in what was going on here and he would have connections to dig deeper legally.

There was no way Garrett was going in this place lone-wolf style. There was too much at stake between his father's case and brown eyes back at the gift shop. Damiani's lead turned out to be hot.

The long windy drive kicked up a dust storm on the way out.

"Those bastards," was all he said, all he could say when he made it back to the highway.

"I couldn't agree more," Brianna conferred. "That poor little girl."

Before he could ask Brianna to, she located his cell and called Colton. They filled his brother in on the scene and Colton promised to get to the bottom of it. He also promised to tread lightly after hearing about security.

"They most likely took a picture of my plates," Garrett said as they rounded out the conversation.

"Why don't you stop by the ranch and pick up a new truck? We can leave that one on the property where no one will be the wiser," Colton said.

"I like the idea, but I better get Brianna back home. She didn't sleep last night after working a long shift," he said.

"Send me her address and we'll send someone out to make the exchange," Colton offered. "That way, you'll have one less thing to worry about."

"I appreciate it," Garrett said. He could get used

to this. He thought about Brianna. As an only child, she didn't have anyone who had her back. Well, not until now. Not until him.

"I'll ask one of the guys to swing by. How far are you away from Brianna's house?" Colton asked.

"A few hours, give or take."

"If one of the guys leaves now, he'll be pretty close to meeting you at her apartment," Colton said.

"Sounds like a plan." Garrett ended the call after thanking his brother.

"Any word on Code Blue?" Brianna asked.

"Not yet. We can swing by the shop if you want but I'd rather get you home and in bed," he said before catching himself. "You know what I mean."

She laughed after she suppressed a yawn. She leaned her head back. "I might not make it all the way home."

"Go ahead and close your eyes. I'll be here when you wake up."

"Thank you for saying that." The look she shot him next would stick with him for a long while.

He meant it.

THE NEXT TIME Brianna opened her eyes, she was somehow in her own bed. The shades were drawn and the room dark. How long had she been out?

Her alarm clock had been turned toward the wall, she figured to block any possible light source. She reached over to turn it around as she tried to clear the fog in her brain. This was the first deep sleep she'd had in too long.

The difference? Garrett O'Connor.

This was the first time she'd been able to relax long enough to really sleep. Being shocked awake felt like she was stuck between conscious and unconscious worlds, somewhere in the middle without committing to either side. Moving felt like sludging through quicksand.

She tossed off the covers and then threw her legs over the side of the bed. She sat there for a long moment in an attempt to get her bearings.

The thought of Garrett being in the next room helped to ground her. She listened for any sounds he was still there despite knowing full well he wouldn't leave her. He'd made a promise and no matter how impulsive he could be, she'd never known him to break his word once given. He might have been a lot of things: rogue, self-centered, misguided, a hothead, but the man's word was as good as gold.

For a moment, she thought about calling out to him for reassurance. Instead, she pushed up to standing, steadied herself and managed to make it to the bathroom without falling over. Coffee would help with the brain fog and she trusted Garrett to be in the next room.

Trust. There was a word. Brianna didn't realize how little she'd grown to trust anyone until recently. Had she shut everyone out? She could say with one hundred percent certainty she kept everyone at arm's length. It was strange because she didn't even realize it had become her habit until Garrett showed up. Even with their history, she was having a difficult time letting him get close. Well, there was physical closeness and the emotional kind. The physical variety didn't seem to be a problem for either one of them. She felt her cheeks flush just thinking about it.

After splashing cold water on her face and then freshening up, she managed to get enough of her bearings to head for the coffee maker. Stepping into the main living area sent her pulse racing. Seeing Garrett sitting at her table, shirtless, was enough to clear the cobwebs.

"Hey there," he said and his voice was low and husky. On a good day, it rippled over her and through her. Now his deep baritone vibrated to her core.

"Hi," was all she could manage as she passed by him. At the very least she managed a smile. Before she stepped into the kitchen area, the aroma of freshly made coffee hit her. "Ah, that smells like heaven."

"Brewed it a couple of minutes ago," he said and she could hear the smile come through his voice despite having her back turned to him.

"Do you ever sleep?" The man was a machine.

"I dozed off a few minutes here and there," he said.

"You're amazing," she said before realizing she actually said the words out loud.

He laughed.

"Have you taken a look at yourself lately?" he asked. "Not only are you putting yourself through school, but you work a job that would put most people under from the kind of energy it requires. Plus, you make it all look easy. Then, there are your grades."

"How do you know about my grades?" She arched a brow as she filled her favorite mug.

"I know you. Don't deny the fact you're getting all As, Brianna."

"I got a B in history of communication graphics," she admitted, leaning her hip against the counter before taking a sip of coffee. Yes, coffee. The caffeine kicked in almost immediately. Or maybe it was Garrett who had her heart racing.

"Not because you couldn't ace the class, I bet." His confidence in her sent more of that warmth spiraling through her.

"I overslept the test and didn't have enough time to answer all the questions," she said with a shrug. "I realized right then how quickly things could go down the drain. Some professors are hard-core and won't take any excuses or allow for makeups no matter what the situation is. Not that I can blame them. I'm sure they've heard every excuse in the book."

"I can only imagine. Makes it hard when someone makes a legitimate mistake and needs a hand," he said, picking up his own cup of coffee and taking a sip. She remembered the taste of coffee on his tongue. Somehow, it tasted so much better that way.

"I managed to get through it and I learned not to go to sleep after a shift when I have a test the next morning," she mused.

"Life isn't always fair. Doesn't mean we have to repeat the same mistakes over and over," he agreed, smiling. "I'm figuring that one out now, so it's never too late to learn."

She realized he must be talking about his family.

"I'm happy you guys are getting on better footing," she said. "You have a great family, Garrett. It would be a shame not to realize it."

"I realized it a little too late with my dad." The smile faded and she saw hurt in its place. "Don't want the same thing to happen with Colton and the others."

"Speaking of Colton, have you heard from him again today?" She glanced at the clock and most of the day was already gone. It was supper time but her internal clock was a mess. She wasn't hungry yet. Maybe after coffee.

"Only to say the information we gave him will help bust up some kind of ring. The details aren't solidified yet. The law will be able to get a warrant to search the place based on the nonprofit application being in dead-people's names and social security numbers," he said, clenching his back teeth.

"You saved that little girl's life. You know that, don't you?" She sure hoped so.

He shrugged. "Not yet."

"She might still be there for a few more hours or maybe a day but I highly doubt law enforcement is going to move slowly now that they have a warrant to search the premises. That's not exactly easy to get. Plus, we played it cool today. We didn't give anything away." She couldn't stress that enough.

Garrett nodded.

"I'm guessing you would feel better if you personally ripped the people responsible into shreds but we both know it would only feel good for a little while.

Knowing they'll end up behind bars for the rest of their lives where they belong is the best possible punishment for those bastards and the only way for justice to be served." She bit back a curse.

"You're right. I know you are." He closed and opened his fingers a few times like he was attempting to work off the stress he felt at thinking about the girl.

"If it makes you feel any better, we can follow up with Colton about her once this is all said and done," she offered.

"I would like that," he said. Some of the tension eased from his face. His shoulders relaxed a little.

"Okay then. What's next? Should we swing by Derk's place?" That reminded her of something else. "Oh, wait. What about Code Blue? Did you get an estimate of when she'd be ready?"

When he smiled this time, it was practically ear to ear.

"She'll be good to go by Monday," he said. "There's a fair amount of work to be done and they have to order a new part, which is the main holdup. But, she'll purr like a kitten—" he flashed eyes at her "—or roar like a mountain lion in your case when they're finished with her."

Brianna beamed.

"I can't thank you enough for your generosity," she said. It still hurt a little bit to accept help of this magnitude but she was determined to get better at it. Because leaning on someone else for a change and being there for them in return made the world feel a whole lot lighter. No matter what else happened and how much her heart begged for more, she hoped she and Garrett would stay close when all this was said and done. She hadn't realized how much she missed having someone in her life until now. She was going out on a limb here but decided Garrett was worth taking the risk.

"You've helped me in so many ways over the past couple of days that it's the least I can do." The sincerity in his words touched her heart.

There wasn't much more to do than smile in return.

"You asked about Derk before we got off on a tangent." He steered the conversation back on course, which was probably for the best. She didn't need to get too caught up in emotions. She made better choices when she used logic and not her heart.

"Right. Should we swing by his place? Maybe talk to him or see what he drives?" she asked.

"Sure. Check out his living situation and see if there even is a way to determine what kind of vehicles he has access to," Garrett said. "But first, we need to get something in your stomach."

"I can grab a quick—"

"Or, I can cook something here." Garrett cut her off midsentence. "I know you're running on *E* most of the time because you have more than a full plate with school and work, but I'd like it if you slowed down."

She was mounting a defense when his hands came up to stop her.

"I think I know what you're about to say and, believe me, I see how you're moving mountains and that means taking advantage of as many hours a day as possible, but you're important to me and I would like to request that you make time to eat," he said in more of a plea than anything else.

The rebuttal died on her tongue. He was right and she could clearly see he was coming from a place of caring. Genuine concern was hard to fight.

"I'm really close to the end of the road with my degree," she said. "I have bills to pay between now and then and a job to find. But, I promise to do my best. Everything you just said is a big part of the reason I've worked my behind off to finish my degree. Believe me when I say that I want to take better care of myself. I realize how much I've been shortchanging that department and I'm so close to the finish line that I can almost taste it."

"I can arrange for a meal service for the next thirty-five days. I heard about it from one of the guys at my last job. He called them divorced-man meals. Said his brother got a delivery every two weeks and the food was good," he said.

She could fight his generosity, or she could take it as a sign the universe wanted to help her out. She chose to see it as the latter.

"Okay," she said.

"Okay?" he parroted. The shock on his face was worth it.

"You heard me," she teased, trying to lighten the mood that had taken a serious turn. "Or do I have to repeat myself?"

Garrett flashed those pearly whites.

"I heard you fine the first time," he quipped. "And

now that we've established that, how about you open the fridge and pick out a meal before we head out."

She should probably be frustrated that he'd gone ahead with his plan while she was asleep. Except that she wouldn't change him even if she could. He would always be a little impulsive and a whole lot of dangerous to her heart.

She sighed. Too bad they couldn't be more than friends.

Chapter Twenty

The drive past campus was filled with easy conversation. They were in a sleek new truck, courtesy of Colton, who'd had it delivered while Brianna rested. Garrett couldn't deny how much he liked being with Brianna. The fact she was willing to let him offer a hand up meant a lot. She wouldn't accept help from just anyone. She could be stubborn when she wanted to be, but he respected her for wanting to do it on her own.

He could relate a little too much to the need for someone to find their own way.

Derk's place was a small duplex. Her classmate's blue hatchback was parked out front. The street was lined with vehicles, some of which were trucks, so it would be impossible to tell if he had access to any one of them.

The only way to find out was to ask.

Garrett parked as close to the white aluminum siding unit as he could manage, which ended up being three duplexes down. He reached for Brianna's hand

and linked their fingers without giving it a thought as they walked on the cracked sidewalk.

On the porch, Garrett rapped on the door three times in police-raid fashion. That should get attention. He was used to his physical size being intimidating to most guys and he wasn't afraid to use the advantage on Derk. At the very least, the guy creeped Brianna out. Garrett intended to make certain Derk walked on the opposite side of the street if he saw her coming after tonight.

An annoyed-looking man jerked the door open. Anger caused his eyebrows to look like slashes. Once he got a good look at who was standing on the other side of the door, he chilled considerably.

"What are you doing here?" His gaze bounced from Garrett to Brianna and back. He seemed especially keen to keep an eye on Garrett. Good. The guy knew where his biggest threat came from.

"You're asking the wrong question, Derk," Garrett practically growled. He was intentionally intimidating him.

"What?" Derk was on the tall side but willowy. He had dark circles underneath his eyes and looked like he'd been staring at a screen too long.

"You should be asking how I know where you live," Garrett said to eyes that grew wider by the second.

"How do yo—"

"Who is there?" a male voice called from somewhere behind Derk.

"Don't worry about it. It's for me," Derk yelled back.

"That's a boldface lie and we both know—"

The door cracked open a little bit more and a second young man appeared. He quickly sized Garrett up. His gaze never left once it locked on. "Can I help you, sir?"

This fellow seemed to know when to show respect.

"Yeah, can you tell me which vehicle belongs to this guy? He doesn't seem to want to cooperate," Garrett said.

The man looked at Derk like he was an alien.

"Sure. He owns the blue hatchback." He stepped out onto the porch and then pointed at the exact vehicle Garrett had seen in the parking lot yesterday. "Why? Did he hit your car and take off or something?"

The guy jabbed Derk in the shoulder. He was clearly a bully and Derk seemed used to taking it.

"Are you two related?" Garrett wondered what kind of man would purposely live with someone who clearly couldn't stand him.

"Not by blood," the guy said. "I'm Everett Fulton, by the way."

Everett stuck out his hand, so Garrett shook it. The fellow had a firm handshake. The kid looked like he worked construction with his jeans and flannel shirt.

"Derk is my stepbrother and our parents cosigned for me to rent this place, so they forced me to take him as a roommate while he's in school up the road," Everett said.

"Which one of these vehicles belongs to you?" Garrett asked.

"I'm the truck right there." He pointed to a late-model Dodge Ram that was practically covered in dents and dirt.

"Does your brother, sorry, stepbrother ever borrow your truck?" Garrett couldn't see Everett handing over the keys, but he had to ask.

"Hell, no. I wouldn't let him drive a go-kart if my life depended on it." Everett scrunched up his face like he'd just bitten into a sour grape.

"Does anyone else live here?" Garrett asked. So far, Everett was an open book.

"No. Just him and me. My girl stays over sometimes but she doesn't live here." His gaze finally slid over to Brianna but quickly snapped back like a soldier at attention.

"You should speak to your brother here about why he dropped out of school." Garrett had no idea if it was a true statement but he figured this was the best way to find out.

Derk had been a little too quiet up until now and he couldn't seem to look Brianna in the eyes. He'd tucked his hands in his pockets and stared at the cement porch until now.

"I didn't quit school," he quickly defended. "I only dropped one class."

Garrett wasn't sure what to think of Derk. There was something off about the young man. Pinning down exactly what it was turned out to be the difficult part. Was he just a creep? Or something more dangerous? Did he just rub people the wrong way? Was he the result of being bullied for much of his life?

He glared at Garrett while he stood there sulking. He was like a little kid who'd gotten yelled at for not cleaning his room. He lacked maturity, and by the looks of him, self-discipline. None of which made him a criminal exactly.

"What the hell, Derk?" Everett whirled around on Derk. "Your mom and my dad are going to cut you off this time."

"This time?" Garrett figured he might as well ask. Everett seemed more than willing to share information with a stranger.

"He pulled this once before. Claimed he got his heart broken by some chick and had to drop out when in reality he got a restraining order against him." Everett looked disgusted. He fisted his hands at his sides. From the looks of him, he was a real hothead. Would Derk stand up to his stepbrother? It didn't appear so.

"We've taken up enough of your time." Though Garrett couldn't imagine Derk standing up to his stepbrother to ask to use the truck, something clearly was off here. He had a restraining order against him, and access to a truck. They had to pursue this lead further, but right now, he wanted to get Brianna safely away.

"Cool. Thanks for the heads-up about school. I'll let our parents know what he's up to when they think he's in class," Everett said.

Garrett shook the kid's hand one more time before giving Derk a stern look. He looked like he might jump out of his own skin to get away from Garrett if he said boo.

Garrett stared straight into Derk's eyes. "If you happen to be 'borrowing' your stepbrother's truck to follow women who don't want to be followed, your parents won't be the only ones after you. Are we clear?"

Derk diverted his gaze and offered a slight nod.

Brianna had been quiet the whole time and he figured she had a reason. Once they got to the vehicle, she said, "I still don't trust him."

"Can't disagree with you there," he said. "I'm not sure he's bold enough to go for the attacks you've had."

"True. I didn't get that sense either." She climbed into the cab and he closed the door behind her.

Once he claimed the driver's seat, he asked, "What do you think about heading back to your place and then hitting up campus again in the morning?"

"It's a good idea," she said. "I made a decision about Professor Jenkins." She paused for a moment while he navigated off the tight road and onto a major street that led to the highway.

"Oh yeah?"

"I'm turning him in. You were right. Graduation on the line or not, I can't allow him to pull this with others. My silence might enable him to continue preying on women. How could I sleep at night if I knowingly let that happen?" she asked, but it was more statement than question.

"You know I'll support you in any way that I can. If you want legal help, our family attorney will be at your beck and call," he said. "He's on retainer and gets paid no matter what so it would give him something to do."

"Doesn't he specialize in cattle ranches and wills?" She raised an eyebrow when he glanced over at her.

"Probably. Shows you how much I know about the legal system," he admitted. He'd been thrown behind bars a time or two for being rowdy and not knowing when to keep his mouth closed but he had no idea how the family business operated on the office end of the house. There weren't many who could claim to know ranching from a ranch hand's point of view better than him, though.

"I appreciate the offer and I might have to take you up on it if this goes south. I'm hoping it doesn't and I finish out the semester without any hiccups. I can file a formal complaint with the university and I'm guessing with the law," she said.

"You'd be within the statute of limitations, considering the incident only just happened." He parked in a different spot despite driving a different truck. It was good to mix it up. Someone could recognize him. Although, having a dedicated parking spot next to Brianna's was looking better and better to him lately.

The few kisses they'd shared kept cycling back in his thoughts. All he could think was...*more*. He wanted more than an occasional scorching-hot kiss that promised to heat up if they took it a step further. He wanted more than stealing a moment here and there. He wanted more than friendship with her.

But that was probably the best way to ruin what they had, whatever it was that was budding between them. Because it was a helluva lot more than friendship on his end. He'd realized that as soon as she'd uttered the word. He'd been kidding himself thinking he could hit the road after taking care of her problem.

BRIANNA HAD BARELY WALKED inside her apartment when her cell phone started buzzing. Her first thought was her boss. Did her work replacement bail without telling her? The all-too-familiar sinking feeling in the pit of her stomach kicked in.

She located her cell inside her purse as Garrett closed and locked the door behind them. He stood at the door, looking ready for just about anything.

She checked the screen, and then shrugged. "I don't recognize the number."

"Answer it anyway and put it on speaker just in case," he offered.

"Right. Good idea," she said, doing just that. "Hello?"

"Is this Brianna Adair?"

She immediately recognized the voice as Blaine's, the TA.

"Yes, how did you get my phone number?" she asked, not looking at Garrett. She could feel anger coming off him in palpable waves.

"Sorry. Please don't get mad. Or worse yet, get me in trouble," Blaine pleaded.

"You're going to have to tell me what this is about first." There was no way she was making a deal before she knew why he called.

"This isn't about me or your grades," he quickly said. "Don't worry there."

"Then, what?" She risked a glance at Garrett. His arms were folded across his muscled chest. She had no doubt he could snap into position and throw a punch before someone had a chance to register that he'd even moved.

"I just wanted to explain something, but, like it's weird over the phone. You know?" He fell silent, no doubt waiting for a response.

"Since I don't know what you're talking about, I can't say that I do know, Blaine." She glanced up at Garrett, who was nodding for her to go along with it.

"It's sensitive. But there's something I think you should know." He paused a second. "My last class of the night wraps in half an hour. Can you meet me?"

"On campus? Yes. How about your office?" she asked.

"No." He sounded off. Nervous. "What about the parking lot? There's some stuff going on and I think you should know about it."

"Not the parking lot, Blaine," she said.

"You pick a place then. Anywhere but my office," he said.

"How about the lawn by the fountain?" The area was well lit and campus police was never far.

Blaine hesitated for a long moment.

"It's there or your office. Take it or leave it." She wasn't in the mood to play games if he was trying to be cute and ask her out.

"Fine. I'll meet you there." He sounded resigned. "Half an hour."

"I'll be there," she said before ending the call. She immediately caught Garrett's gaze. "We can make it if we hurry."

Chapter Twenty-One

Garrett made it to campus in what Brianna described as record time. He parked the truck and then watched as she bolted toward the lawn. He let her get a solid head start before pulling up the map of campus on his cell and studying the best vantage point.

In a public place, he wasn't worried about Brianna being able to handle herself for a few minutes. She'd explained campus security was good about being visible during class changes. Since this was the last class of the night, there would be plenty of security around. He could use it to his advantage.

In fact, one had just driven behind Garrett and he half expected the vehicle to stop and question him. Class was almost out and he could be picking someone up, so the vehicle kept moving at a snail's pace, winding through the lot. *Good.*

The thought of Brianna walking out to Code Blue every night alone didn't sit well with him. He didn't even want to imagine her driving home in something as unreliable as her Jeep. Come Monday, part of the problem would be solved when she got Code Blue back in tip-top shape. From what the mechanic said, she was lucky it had held out this long.

Garrett had to hand it to her. She didn't give up easily. Most would let the first setback throw them off course. What she was doing was truly heroic in his book. And he was damn proud of the woman she'd become. From a place deep inside him, he wanted to prove he was worthy of her.

He had no idea where the thought came from but, for the first time, he didn't want to shove it aside. He wanted to figure out exactly what it meant and then see if she could possibly feel the same way.

Right now, he had another priority. Keep her alive.

There were four buildings directly on the lawn. One had a coffee shop. It would have been an ideal place to watch from if it was open. A few people started milling toward the parking lot. He was about to be salmon swimming upstream.

Dodging through throngs of young adults, he managed to make it to the Administration Building. He stood with his back against the bricks near the corner. From his peripheral, he could see Brianna sitting on the fountain's edge, waiting.

A nervous-looking guy approached her as Garrett bummed a cigarette off a student walking by. "You have a light?"

"Yeah, sure." The guy pulled out a lighter and flicked it.

Garrett didn't smoke but holding a lit cigarette would provide cover for him standing there rather than heading straight to his vehicle like everyone else. As the sea of students thinned, he leaned his head back against the bricks and faked taking a drag.

Most people weren't all that observant. They noticed broad strokes, not details. He hoped the same was true for Blaine.

From this distance, he couldn't hear a word being said and he didn't like being in the dark.

Brianna threw her arms up in the air, looking frustrated, and Garrett had to remind himself to stay planted. He needed to play it cool or blow his cover. Was this the guy who'd been stalking her? His thoughts snapped to other possibilities. So far, Derk was his top suspect.

Derk wouldn't *ask* his stepbrother to borrow his truck. He would take it out in the middle of the night without permission knowing full well Everett would rather die than give Derk the keys. The truck already had a few bumps and bruises being a basic work vehicle used in construction.

The way Derk had stood there sulking didn't sit well with Garrett. The blue hatchback at the bar could have been him scoping out the scene, making certain there wasn't extra security or any cops.

There'd been something about the expression on Derk's face that had Garrett thinking. He'd looked like he was doing more than sulking. He'd looked smug. *Dammit.*

It took everything inside Garrett not to shout over to Brianna. He was pretty certain he needed to act fast, and they'd let themselves get distracted with this Blaine fellow. Garrett bit out a few more curses before stubbing the cigarette out on the wall. He cupped the butt in his hand so he could toss it in the trash once it cooled down.

Brianna started to walk away from Blaine. He grabbed her arm. *Wrong move, buddy.*

Garrett didn't even have a chance to move before Brianna snapped her arm down, freeing herself. She spun around and poked her finger in Blaine's chest as she bawled him out. Garrett could hear her voice even though he couldn't quite make out the words.

He pulled on every ounce of self-control to stand there while she finished chewing the guy out. It was clear to see she was fully capable of sticking up for herself. And yet, Garrett still wanted to show Blaine just how uncool it was to put his hands on her without her permission.

This time, when she stalked off Blaine seemed to know better. He stood there, looking dumbfounded. Garrett rolled toward the parking lot and started a slow walk in case he needed to double back. Until recently, he wouldn't have been able to control his temper. This was progress. He had to admit life ran smoother when he took a minute before reacting and he had the added benefit of making better decisions.

Brianna fumed as she approached the truck.

"What happened back there?" he asked.

"Mind if we do this inside the truck?" She didn't wait for an answer. She marched toward the passenger side where he stood. He opened the door, and then made his way over to the driver's seat.

He started the ignition, ready to circle back to Derk's house to talk to Everett a little more, figuring there was no way Derk was still there.

"That jerk just basically begged me not to get his boss Professor Jenkins in trouble by turning him in." Her fisted hands sat on top of her thighs. "Can you believe that garbage?"

Before he could formulate a response, she continued, "The nerve of him. I don't care if Jenkins is in the middle of a messy divorce. If he's hitting on students, his wife *should* leave him."

"How did Blaine know what happened?" Garrett asked.

"Jenkins must have told him. Blaine went on about how Jenkins could come off the wrong way at times, but he didn't mean any harm…*any harm*." She blew out a frustrated-sounding breath as she repeated those last words. "If they think I was born yesterday or that I'm so special I'm the only one he's tried this on, they have another think coming."

"Do you suspect either of them is capable of stalking you with the truck?" Garrett gripped the steering wheel.

"I asked what kind of vehicles they drove," she admitted. "Neither one has a truck. Blaine is driving his mother's old sedan and Jenkins drives a luxury car."

"I believe we need to move faster on Derk," he said. "I couldn't shake the smug look he wore during the visit. Like he was getting something over on all of us."

"He was. He gave me chills." She turned to face Garrett before sucking in a breath. "He's the one who makes the most sense, isn't he?"

"It's looking very much like he had access to a truck," he said.

"Which had quite a few bumps and bruises on it already, not to mention the fact it was covered in dust and dirt."

"Making it easier to hide more scrapes and scratches," Garrett figured.

She smacked the flats of her palms on her thighs. "Before we do anything else, though, I need to report Professor Jenkins."

"A trip to local law enforcement should do the trick after you report him to campus administration," he said. "What are your thoughts on Blaine? Have you ruled him out?"

"I think I have. He's a coward and would do anything Professor Jenkins asked. Blaine hit on me before, but I think he took my rejection seriously and moved on," she said.

"Good. At least the man has some sense. Asking you not to turn in his boss isn't his best move." Garrett twisted the key in the ignition…nothing happened. He cursed as he scanned the area, looking for the hatchback. Derk had to have been the one who'd messed with the battery cables on Garrett's truck at the bar last night. Was he showing off? Proving he could get to Garrett?

"What is it? What's wrong?" Concern brought her voice up a couple of octaves.

"My guess? Derk. He's the reason I was late following you last night. Your friend Hammer held me up and Derk took advantage of the distraction to loosen my battery cables so my truck wouldn't start. It gave him the head start he needed to get to you before I could." Garrett issued a sharp sigh.

"We can always ask for a jump from security," she offered.

"It's not the battery this time. There would be a click, click, click sound. He's doing something else." Garrett held up his phone. "Would you mind texting Colton and letting him in on what's going on while I pop the hood?"

She took the cell with a nod, and then started typing while he exited the truck after unlocking the hood. He figured there had to be a flashlight somewhere in the vehicle. As he rounded the driver's side, his gut clenched.

Brianna was on her way out of the truck with a gun pointed directly at her temple.

"You better stop right there or I'll squeeze this trigger and you'll be picking her brains out of this truck for years to come," Derk said in a high-pitched squeal.

Brianna mouthed, "I'm sorry."

He gave a quick head shake to let her know he didn't for one second believe this was her fault as he put his hands in the air so Derk could see them. If Garrett had his own truck he would know exactly where he kept a backup pistol. He always had a weapon on him while working ever since he was attacked by a coyote at the tender age of nine years old. He still had a scar on his back from turning in the opposite direction and trying to run. If Colton hadn't been nearby and heard Garrett scream, he most likely wouldn't be standing here today.

"Whoa there." Garrett used as calm a voice as possible. Brianna's life depended on it.

"Everyone is always making fun of Derk." The fact he referred to himself in third person wasn't real reassuring as to his mental fitness. "But I'm showing all of you."

"You haven't done anything that can't be undone yet," Garrett said.

"How little you know about me and yet you're talking like you have it all figured out," Derk said. "It's too late now. I'm forced to act much earlier than I'd planned."

He had a plan? Garrett couldn't for the life of him figure out what that meant.

"There's no way he's kicking me out. I won't have it. This had to be done. I won't be taken advantage of again." His gaze narrowed as he used Brianna as a human shield. Even if Garrett had a weapon there was no clean shot.

Derk forced them back a couple of steps, making it difficult for Garrett to see them.

"Don't do this. Whatever you have planned. It's not too late to back out of—"

A wicked-sounding snort tore from Derk's throat. "You have no idea what I'm capable of."

And then it dawned on Garrett.

Everett was probably dead, unconscious, tied up. Something that got him out of the way. The plan. Derk used his stepbrother's truck to harass Brianna and then got him out of the way. But what did he plan to do with…

No. No. No.

The pieces clicked together in Garrett's mind. Murder-suicide.

"But now you're in the way and I have to deal with you too." Derk was almost hysterical as he spoke. "It wasn't supposed to go down like this but what do we do when things don't go our way? We don't scrap the whole plan. We pivot. Ask Mom. She's always talking about making sure we pivot. It's what she did when she married that horrible father of Everett's. Honestly, Everett didn't deserve to live."

Brianna gasped. The terrified look on her face said she'd pieced together the whole plan. Garrett's worst-case scenario was true.

"That's right. I'm the complication. You should probably deal with me first." Garrett would trade his own life to free Brianna. A lightning bolt struck his heart in that moment and he realized how much he couldn't lose her. He had no idea how she felt about him beyond a handful of kisses so hot they could melt metal. But he intended to find out. Because if he had even the slightest chance with her, he had no intention of blowing it this time.

First, he had to find a way to keep her alive.

Derk's face morphed into a scowl.

"You're nothing." He aimed the gun toward Garrett.

In that moment, Brianna made her move. She dropped down, taking his arm with her. The next thing he heard over a few grunts was the sound of metal scraping against concrete. Without hesitation, Garrett barreled around the front of the borrowed truck as the sound of sirens split the air.

Derk threw Brianna aside, his gaze frantic as he searched for the gun. Her head hit the concrete hard, but she bounced right back up and clawed at Derk the second he located the weapon.

Too bad, Garrett was there first anyway. He threw the gun as far as he could before spinning around and diving toward Derk, who was pushing to stand. Garrett dove straight into Derk's knees, and then heard a snap.

Derk cried out in pain as Brianna ran to get the weapon.

"No. No. This can't be happening." Derk bit and scratched and screamed, but he was no match for Garrett. He pinned the kid's arms to his sides and then slammed him on his stomach.

A few seconds later, Brianna stood five feet away, feet spread apart, aiming the gun at Derk.

"You're going to jail for a very long time. I hope you like being locked up with men twice your size and ten times your strength. You thought Everett was bad…just wait until you're locked up in maximum-security prison." Blood trickled down the side of her forehead.

"I got this guy." Garrett tried to soothe. "You can sit down if you want to."

"I'm good, Garrett."

She fainted at the moment a squad car screeched onto the scene.

Chapter Twenty-Two

"What happened?" Brianna came to in Garrett's arms. She blinked up at him as her mind started clicking through the evening's events.

"You decided to take a nap," Garrett teased but worry lines etched his forehead.

"Where am I?"

"The back of an ambulance," he supplied. "Someone has been waiting for you to wake up."

An EMT came into view from around the back of the ambulance. He asked a couple of questions and shone a small light in her eyes. She must have passed his tests because he smiled and nodded at Garrett.

"Everett?" she asked.

"Derk killed him using the gun he intended to shoot you with. There was a suicide note in the duplex that explained how Derk was in love with you and you kept rejecting him. It went on to say that if he couldn't have you no one would." Garrett stopped for a second like he needed a minute before continuing.

Losing a young life was so tragic. Brianna's heart went out to the kid's parents and friends. Based on the look on Garrett's face, he was processing the same way as she was…such a shame.

"Derk had on gloves. I'm not sure if you noticed that," he said.

"If I did, I don't remember," she admitted.

"You took a pretty big blow to the head when you fought him," Garrett said. "I've never been prouder of you, though. And I'm just so relieved you're all right."

He stopped like he needed to catch his breath.

"The timing of this is terrible. I know. But I don't want to wait another minute to know where I stand with you," he said.

Her breath caught and her pulse kicked up a few notches.

"I've realized over the past couple of days what has been missing in my life, which is ironic because I've never believed I needed anyone but myself to be fine. And then I ran into you at that gas station, looking like the sexiest drowned rat I've ever seen." Garrett broke into a small smile at the memory before continuing. "And I've come to know just how much you mean to me." He caught her gaze and held it. "I'm head over heels in love with you, Bri. And I'm asking if there's any chance, no matter how slight, that you might feel the same way."

He closed his eyes and took in a breath.

"Open your eyes, Garrett. I want you to be looking at me when I say this," she said.

He obliged.

"I think I've been in love with you since that first day of middle school when you took the seat next to me and introduced yourself. I know we hit some bumps in the road but seeing you again, being around you again, has only confirmed what I think I always knew down deep. There was never anyone else for me than you. I'm in love with you, Garrett. And I'd like to find a way to build a life together."

"You mean that?" His ear-to-ear smile overtook any hesitation he might have been feeling a few seconds ago.

"With my whole heart."

He bent down and pressed the most tender kiss on her lips she'd ever felt. So tender, it robbed her breath.

He opened his eyes.

"Marry me, Bri. Make me the happiest man in the world."

She was already nodding her answer before he finished his sentence. "Yes, Garrett. I would love to marry you. I think you're the reason I wanted to go back to Katy Gulch all these years. My heart needed to be near you."

Garrett placed a few more tender kisses on her lips before pressing his forehead to hers. "I promise to give you all of me. I promise to always take a few breaths before responding. And I promise to love you for the rest of my life."

"I'll take that vow," she said before reaching up to plant a few of her own kisses.

GARRETT PACKED THE LAST of Brianna's things into box number fifty-four. Her apartment was almost ready to go as she finished her last final. He'd moved in temporarily, but they were both ready to relocate back to the family ranch where he could step into his role in the family business.

The past thirty-some-odd days had gone by in a flash. He was set to claim their life together. Brianna had volunteered to take on the family's website but her heart was in teaching tech to underprivileged kids. She'd signed up to volunteer in Austin once a week and there was a whole lot she wanted to do locally along with some work on the ranch.

Garrett's cell buzzed and he hoped it was the call he'd been waiting for.

A quick glance at the screen said it was Colton.

"Hey, I have good news." Colton started right in.

"Okay." Garrett didn't want to get too worked up before he had confirmation.

"Missy, the abused girl from the alpaca farm, has been placed in your care while they try to locate her parents," Colton said with the kind of pride that made Garrett's chest swell.

"We're official? The foster thing went through even though we're not married yet?"

"I vouched on your behalf as did all of our brothers. We're a compelling team when we decide to get something done," Colton said.

"That we are, brother. That we are." Garrett couldn't wait to tell Brianna the minute she walked through the door. Neither of them had felt right about leaving that little girl in the gift shop that day about a month ago. Now they would care for her while she healed and they launched a proper search for her birth parents.

"Besides, it'll be good practice for both of you," Colton teased.

"Let us tie the knot before we start talking about having a family," he shot back. But with Missy coming into their lives and staying as long as she needed to, and having found Brianna, he knew in his heart that his family was already here. There was plenty of time to discuss having kids of their own someday when they were both ready. As for now, they were home.

* * * * *

Don't miss the conclusion of
An O'Connor Family Mystery series from
USA TODAY *bestselling author Barb Han when*
Texas Abduction *goes on sale in December 2021!*

And if you missed the previous books in the series,
look for:

Texas Kidnapping
Texas Target
Texas Law
Texas Baby Conspiracy

Available now wherever
Harlequin Intrigue books are sold!

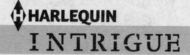
#2037 TARGETING THE DEPUTY
Mercy Ridge Lawmen • by Delores Fossen

After narrowly escaping an attempt on his life, Deputy Leo Logan is shocked
to learn the reason for the attack is his custody battle for his son with his ex,
Olivia Nash. To catch the real killer, he'll have to keep them both close—and risk
falling for Olivia all over again.

#2038 CONARD COUNTY: CHRISTMAS BODYGUARD
Conard County: The Next Generation • by Rachel Lee

Security expert Hale Scribner doesn't get personal with clients. Ever. But having
evidence that could put away a notoriously shady CEO doesn't make Allie Burton
his standard low-risk charge. With an assassin trailing them 24/7, they'll need a
Christmas miracle to survive the danger...and their undeniable attraction.

#2039 TEXAS ABDUCTION
An O'Connor Family Mystery • by Barb Han

When Cheyenne O'Connor's friend goes missing, she partners with her estranged
husband, rancher Riggs O'Connor, for answers. During their investigation,
evidence emerges suggesting their daughter—who everyone claims died at
childbirth—might be alive and somehow connected. Riggs and Cheyenne are
determined to find out what really happened...and if their little girl will be coming
home after all.

#2040 MOUNTAINSIDE MURDER
A North Star Novel Series • by Nicole Helm

North Star undercover operative Sabrina Killian is on a hit man's trail and doesn't
want help from Wyoming search and rescue ranger Connor Lindstrom. But the
persistent ex-SEAL is the killer's real target. Will Sabrina and Connor's most
dangerous secrets even the odds—or take them out for good?

#2041 ALASKAN CHRISTMAS ESCAPE
Fugitive Heroes: Topaz Unit • by Juno Rushdan

With an elite CIA kill squad locating hacker Zenobia Hanley's Alaska wilderness
hideout, it's up to her mysterious SEAL neighbor, John Lowry, to save her from
capture. Regardless of the risks and secrets they're both hiding, John's determined
to protect Zee because there's more at stake this Christmas than just their lives...

#2042 BAYOU CHRISTMAS DISAPPEARANCE
by Denise N. Wheatley

Mona Avery is determined to investigate a high-profile missing person case in
the Louisiana bayou before heading home for Christmas. Stubborn detective
Dillon Reed insists she's more of a hindrance than a help. But when a killer wants
Mona's story silenced, only Dillon can keep her safe...

---

*When she discovers high-level corruption at her job,
accountant Allie Burton finds herself—reluctantly—in
desperate need of a bodyguard. Tall, ruggedly handsome
and terse, Hale Scribner goes all in to save lives, even if it
means staying on the move, going from town to town. But
once they hit the bucolic Conard County, Allie puts her foot
down and demands a traditional Christmas celebration…
which may be how they lure a killer to his prey…*

Keep reading for a sneak peek at
Conard County: Christmas Bodyguard,
part of Conard County: The Next Generation,
from New York Times *bestselling author Rachel Lee.*

"You need a bodyguard."

Allie Burton's jaw dropped as soon as her dad's old friend Detective
Max Roles spoke the words.

It took a few beats for Allie to reply. "Oh, come on, Max. That's over-
the-top. I'm sure Mr. Ellis was talking about all his international businesses,
about protecting his companies. He said he'd put the auditing firm on it."

Max was getting up in years. His jowls made him look like a bloodhound
with a bald head. Allie had known him all her life, thanks to his friendship
with her father, who had died years ago. She trusted him, but this?

"What were his *exact* words, Allie?"

She pulled them up from recent memory. "He said, *exactly*, that I
shouldn't tell anyone anything about what I'd found in the books."

Max shook his head. "And the rest?"

She shrugged. "He said, and I quote, *Bad things can happen*. Well, of
course they could. He's a tycoon with companies all over the world. Any
irregularity in the books could cause big problems."

"Right," Max said. "I want you to think about that. Bad things can
happen."

Allie frowned. "I guess you're one of the people I shouldn't have told
about this. I thought you'd laugh and wouldn't tell anyone."

"I won't tell anyone except the bodyguard you're going to hire. You've been on the inside of Jasper Ellis's success."

"So what?"

Max leaned forward. "I have nothing against the man's success. We've been investigating him for years, and we've never found a thing we could hang on him. He's good at covering evidence."

"You've been investigating him for what?"

Max blew a cloud. "For the unexplained disappearances and supposed suicides of a number of his employees."

Allie felt a chill run down her spine. Her own dismissal of the situation began to feel naive. "You're kidding," she murmured.

"I wish I was. Here's the thing. At first it could be dismissed. But then the numbers really caught our attention and we started looking into it. Nothing traces directly back to Ellis except he's at the top of the pyramid. You may remember I fought against you going to work for him."

Allie did. Max had strenuously argued with her, something he never did. He was not a man given to conspiracy theories. A hard-nosed detective, he stuck to the facts. He seemed to have some facts right now.

"So I'm going to call that bodyguard. I've known him for years, since he was still in the Marines. I trust him with your life. And you're not leaving my house before he gets here."

"God, Max!"

"Just go make yourself a cup of whatever. But you are *not* going anywhere."

He punctuated those words like bullet shots. Truly shaken, Allie rose to get that drink. She trusted Max. Completely. He'd been like an uncle to her for most of her life. If Max said it, it was true.

As she passed through the short hallway, she saw her reflection in the full-length mirror. Allie paused, wondering who that woman in there was. She felt so changed that she shouldn't look the same. Neat dark blue business slack suit, a blue-striped button-down shirt, collar open. Her ash-blond hair in a fluffed, loose short cut because she didn't feel like fussing with it. A trim every couple of weeks solved that problem.

A bodyguard? The thought sent a tendril of ice creeping along her spine. Seriously?

Don't miss
Conard County: Christmas Bodyguard *by Rachel Lee,*
available December 2021 wherever
Harlequin Intrigue books and ebooks are sold.

Harlequin.com

From *New York Times* bestselling author

B.J. DANIELS

They're running for their lives...and something even more precious...

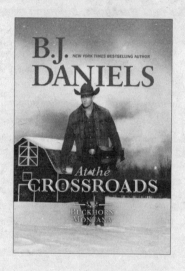

"Daniels is a perennial favorite on the romantic suspense front, and I might go as far as to label her the cowboy whisperer."
—*BookPage* on *Luck of the Draw*

Order your copy today!

HQNBooks.com

SPECIAL EXCERPT FROM

HQN

Meet New York Times *bestselling author B.J. Daniels in*
At the Crossroads,
her next Buckhorn, Montana novel.

Read on for a sneak peek.

At the Crossroads

Bobby Braden wiped the blood off his fingers, noticing that he'd
smeared some on the steering wheel. He pulled his shirtsleeve down
and cleaned the streak of red away, the van swerving as he did.

"Hey, watch it!" In the passenger seat, Gene Donaldson checked
his side mirror. "All we need is for a cop to pull us over," he said in
his deep, gravelly voice. It reminded Bobby of the grind of a chain
saw. "If one of them sees you driving crazy—"

"I got it," he grumbled. "Go back to sleep," he said under his
breath as he checked the rearview mirror. The black line of highway
behind them was as empty as the highway in front of them. There was
no one out here in the middle of Montana on a Sunday this early in
the morning—especially this time of year, with Christmas only weeks
away. He really doubted there would be a cop or highway patrol. But
he wasn't about to argue. He knew that would be his last mistake.

He stared ahead at the narrow strip of blacktop, wondering why
Gene had been so insistent on them coming this way. Shouldn't they
try to cross into Canada? If Gene had a plan, he hadn't shared it. Same
with the bank job that Gene said would be a piece of cake. Unless
an off-duty cop just happened to be in there cashing his check—and
armed.

Concentrating on staying between the lines, Bobby took a breath
and let it out slowly. He could smell the blood and the sweat and the

fresh clean scent that rose from his shirt, which he and the others had stolen off a clothesline somewhere near the border. The shirt was too big, but he'd liked the color. Blue like his eyes. It bothered him that he'd gotten blood on the sleeve. The smear kept catching his eye, distracting him.

At a sound behind him, he glanced in the rearview mirror and saw Eric's anxious face. Bobby regretted letting Eric talk him into this, but he'd needed to get out of the state for a while. Now here he was back in Montana.

"How's Gus?" he asked, keeping his voice down. He could hear Gene snoring but not his usual foghorn sound. Which meant he wasn't completely out yet. Or he could be faking it.

Eric moved closer, pulling himself up with a hand on Bobby's seat as he leaned forward and dropped his voice. "He's not going to make it."

Bobby met his gaze in the rearview for a moment, a silent understanding between them. They both knew what would happen if Gene's younger brother died.

"We aren't leaving Gus behind," Gene said without opening his eyes. "He'll pull through. He's strong." He opened his eyes and looked around. "Where the hell are we?"

"According to the last sign I saw, just outside Buckhorn, Montana," Bobby said.

"Good. There's a café in town. Go there," Gene said, making Bobby realize that had been the man's plan all along. "We'll get food and medical supplies for Gus and dump this van for a different ride." He pulled the pistol from beneath his belt and checked to make sure the clip was full before tucking it under the cotton jacket he'd gotten off the line.

Bobby met Eric's gaze again in the mirror. Things were about to get a whole lot worse.

Available wherever HQN Books are sold.

HQNBooks.com